AMISH WIDOW'S HOPE

EXPECTANT AMISH WIDOWS BOOK 1

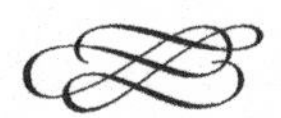

SAMANTHA PRICE

Scripture quotations from The Authorized (King James) Version. Rights in the Authorized Version in the United Kingdom are vested in the Crown. Reproduced by permission of the Crown's patentee, Cambridge University Press.

CHAPTER 1

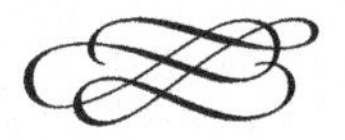

For the righteous Lord loveth righteousness; his countenance doth behold the upright.
Psalm 11:7

Anita turned around from her front-row window seat position, and looked to confirm that she was the only Amish person traveling on the Greyhound bus. This wasn't the first time she'd traveled by Greyhound; the last time she was on one of their buses was when she and her late husband, Joshua, were traveling to his home in Ohio to start their married life together.

Anita had first met Joshua when he'd visited her community in Lancaster County for a few months to help his uncle. She'd had no idea that eight years later, she'd be traveling back without him along the very same route.

Her eyes fell to the bump underneath her dress. Their child would arrive in four months and he or she would be a comfort to her.

After Joshua died, she'd lived alone for three months before her younger brother insisted she move back to Lancaster to live with him and his family.

Anita rested her hands on her swollen belly and wondered why Joshua had been taken from her; it didn't seem right. It had taken them eight years to conceive a baby and the day after they'd found out they were going to be parents, he was taken from her.

He wouldn't be around to see his baby come into the world.

She closed her eyes and relived the day when the police knocked on her door to tell her that a pickup truck had collided with Joshua's buggy. The shock of that moment would be burned into her memory forever. As soon as she'd been told what had happened, everything around her spun and she fell to the floor. It seemed as though she had been in a dream. When she came to, the two police officers standing over her provided unwelcome confirmation that it had been no dream. The policemen had been kind. They had explained that Joshua had been rushed to the hospital, and despite the emergency medical technicians doing all they could he'd died on the way.

She was nineteen-years old when she first laid eyes on Joshua Graber; it was when he'd come to a youth singing with his cousins. As soon as their eyes locked on to one another, there was an instant attraction. He was tall and looked strong; he had a sense of maturity about him which the boys in her community lacked.

"True love is what it was," Anita mumbled to herself before she realized the man sitting next to her probably overheard her. She looked over at the elderly man, and he gave her a quick smile.

Talking to herself was a habit she'd acquired after she'd been living on her own. She didn't see anything wrong with talking to herself. *It's just like thinking thoughts, but said aloud,* she'd tell herself.

Oh, Joshua, I wish you were here with me now. I miss you so much. Anita fought back tears; she'd have to be strong for her baby. She wondered what it would be like for her baby to grow up without a father. When she and Joshua had been hoping and praying for a baby, they never considered for one minute that Joshua might not be around.

Anita was distracted from her thoughts when the man next to her folded his newspaper into his lap and looked at her. "Are you heading home?" he asked.

She smiled at him. She'd rather not talk to anyone, but the man did look kind. "Yes. I'm heading home."

The man smiled at her and gave a slight nod.

The truth was she didn't know where her home was anymore. Was her home with her family, or was her home back in the house that Joshua and she had shared? Anita had to will herself to stop the tears welling in her eyes. If Joshua were still alive, her home would be anywhere he was. With him gone, nowhere seemed like home.

She could see the man wasn't going to stop talking when he said, "Been visiting people, have you?"

"I've been living in Ohio, and now I'm moving back to Lancaster County. My husband died and now I'm going back to live with my brother and his family."

"Ah, I'm very sorry to hear that. Not about living with your brother, I'm sure that's a comfort to you. I'm sorry about you losing your husband." The man looked genuinely sad, which somehow made Anita feel a little better. "I lost my wife a few years ago, so I know what it's like." The man inhaled deeply.

Tears fell down her cheeks. Now she was sad for the man next to her as well as sad for herself. She wiped her wet cheeks with the back of her hand. The man handed her a handkerchief from his pocket.

"Thank you." Anita wiped her eyes and took a deep breath.

"It gets easier over time."

"Does it?"

He nodded. After a moment, he said, "You having a baby?"

She was taken aback by his question; she

wasn't used to discussing her condition with strangers. He'd been the only person who'd guessed she was expecting because her large dresses hid the bump well.

Anita looked down at her belly to see that it was more prominent the way she was sitting. She looked across at him. "Yes. I am."

"Congratulations," he said. "I suppose it's a mixed blessing in a way."

"I guess that's what it is."

Although the man was trying to be kind, his comment made Anita feel even more sorry for herself. Joshua would never play with his baby. *They'll meet in heaven, in Gott's haus,* Anita comforted herself with that thought. "Do you have any children yourself?"

The man's face lit up. "I certainly do. I have three boys. The youngest just turned thirty."

"That's nice." Considering that the man

looked to be in his seventies, she asked. "And grandchildren?"

"None yet." The man chuckled. "I'm hoping they'll settle down soon and have families."

Anita nodded, and then looked straight ahead. She could not think of one man in her community over twenty who was unmarried, except for a couple of older widowers.

"Things will get better for you."

"That's kind of you to say."

He reached out his hand. "I'm Harry Cummings."

Anita shook his hand. "I'm Anita Graber."

"Nice to meet you. Someone once told me something that helped. They told me not to expect things in life to be fair." He wagged a finger. "We expect life to be fair for some unknown reason, but it's not. Sometimes things just don't work out."

"Yes. That does help."

Anita was pleased to have the distraction

when the man went on to talk about all the life lessons he'd learned. She must have fallen asleep because the next thing she knew the bus was making a food stop.

"Anita, do you want to stretch your legs?" Harry asked.

"Yes."

Anita heard that they had a twenty-minute stop. She freshened up and then got something to eat before she got back onto the bus. As she sat munching on a bag of crisps, she wondered what Amos, her brother, would look like now. Would he still be the same gangly boy she'd said goodbye to eight long years ago? She'd met Hannah, the girl Amos had eventually married; the three of them had been in the same group of young people. She had two nephews she'd never met, a two, and a three-year-old.

They were only halfway through their journey and Anita wondered whether she'd ever return to the home she'd just leased out.

Anita glanced at Harry to see that he was glued to a book, and Anita guessed he was all talked out. She folded her black shawl and put it against the window as a pillow. She pressed her head into the soft fabric of the shawl, and then closed her eyes.

CHAPTER 2

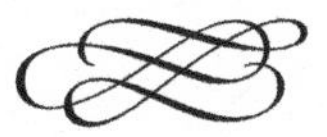

I am not ashamed: for I know whom I have believed, and am persuaded that he is able to keep that
which I have committed unto him against that day.

2 Timothy 1:12

She'd had to change buses for one that would take her closer to home. She'd managed to sleep for a long stretch during the trip and was looking forward to seeing her brother's family.

As soon as the bus stopped, she got off and looked around. Then she saw a large man heading toward her and smiling at her. Gone was the skinny clean-shaven boy she'd left behind.

He hurried to her and took her bag from her. Without hugging her, he asked, "Is this all you have?"

She looked down at the plain brown suitcase. All her furniture and household items had been included with her house when she had leased it out to a young couple. Everything that she could call her own was in that small bag. She looked up at Amos, and nodded. "Doesn't your big *schweschder* deserve a hug after all these years?" She put her arms out toward him.

He smiled, stepped in toward her, and in an awkward manner, put his arm around her to give her a squeeze. "I've got Hannah and the boys waiting in the buggy."

"I'm looking forward to meeting them. Well, meeting the boys, and seeing Hannah again."

Hannah jumped out of the buggy when she saw them approach. Unlike Amos, Hannah threw her arms around Anita. "I'm so pleased you've come, Anita."

"Denke for having me into your home."

"Always."

Anita was pleased with that friendly response feeling a little of the tension finally melt from her body.

"Where are the boys?" Anita said, peeping into the buggy.

"They both fell asleep," Hannah said.

Anita climbed into the back with the boys.

When Hannah had climbed into the front with Amos, she turned around and said, "The bigger one is Ben, and the smaller one is Sam."

"*Jah,* I remember that from the letters. And they've just had their birthdays. Ben is three and Sam is two."

"*Jah,* that's right."

"They're so beautiful," Anita said staring at them.

"They're beautiful when they're asleep," Amos grunted loudly.

Hannah poked her husband. "Hush, Amos. You'll wake them. Don't mind Amos, Anita, they're good boys. They're no trouble at all."

Anita giggled, while Amos took the reins and the buggy rolled forward.

"We've cleaned out the *grossdaddi haus* for you. In exchange for your keep you'll help Hannah with the chores."

"Of course. Naturally I'll help with the chores, but I can pay towards the running of the household. I'm getting money from leasing out my *haus*. I didn't come here to be a burden."

Hannah turned around, and said, "*Nee.* No need to do that. You keep that money for you and the *boppli.*"

"That's a point I'll talk to you about later, Anita," said Amos.

Anita noticed that Hannah shrank low in her seat when Amos glared at her.

"*Jah.* We can talk later, Amos," Anita said.

Hannah said, "I hope you don't mind staying in the *grossdaddi haus.* No one's been in it for years. Or you could stay in the main *haus* with us if you prefer there are plenty of spare rooms."

Amos seemed to be annoyed by his wife. "Anita knows the *haus,* she grew up in it."

"Of course, I'm sorry, Anita."

"No reason to be sorry. The *grossdaddi haus* will be fine. It'll be more than fine."

"See?" Amos said smugly to his wife.

Anita thought it best to keep quiet. She

looked at the sleeping boys and was tempted to poke them so they'd wake up and she could play with them. She'd always wanted to be a mother and Joshua had always wanted to be a father. Anita had often tried to push Joshua out of her mind to stop her hurt, but her swelling belly was a constant reminder of the love that they once shared.

"I'm so glad you've come, Anita. It'll be nice to have a woman around the house; I'm surrounded by boys," Hannah giggled.

"You have friends to the house all the time," Amos said.

Hannah glanced over at Amos and said nothing more.

As soon as the buggy pulled up at the house that Anita had grown up in, she felt a sense of comfort. The boys woke as soon as the buggy stopped. When they opened their eyes, Anita saw that they had the same blue-green eyes as Amos, whereas Hannah's eyes were brown. "They've got the same eyes as their *vadder.*"

"*Jah,* I tell Amos all the time that when we have girls, they'll have the same eyes as mine." Hannah giggled.

Hannah reached in and picked up the bigger of the two boys, and Anita went to pick up the smaller boy.

"*Nee,* Anita, he's too heavy for you."

"It's okay."

"I'll get Amos to carry him into the house."

When both ladies looked around, they saw that Amos was already at the front door of the house. "They're old enough to walk."

"But it's late, and they're so tired."

"You can't spoil them, Hannah. They have to learn to be men."

Anita was not going to interfere in how her brother wanted to raise his children. She was a little worried that her brother seemed to be in a bad mood and she didn't want to cause him any further irritation.

"Amos, will you come and help me in with the boys?" Hannah was evidently growing impatient.

Amos threw down Anita's bag, and stomped back to the buggy.

"I can get Sam, it's okay," Anita said trying to help.

Amos stopped in his tracks. "Anita said she can help you."

"I don't want Anita to lift anything in her condition. Sam's quite heavy."

"Can't you carry him and let Ben walk?" Amos said.

Anita continued, more agitated than before, "Amos, please come here and help! I don't want the boys walking through the mud."

Anita raised her eyebrows and remained silent. Why couldn't her brother do as he was asked.

He continued toward the buggy. "You're right. I'm sorry Anita. I should've thought about that."

"That's all right. No need to be sorry."

Anita continued to the *haus* and overheard Amos say to Hannah, "Well what's she going to do if she can't help you with the boys?"

Hannah answered, "Shh. She'll hear you."

When Amos set Sam down, Hannah walked with Anita through to the *grossdaddi haus.* "You should be quite comfortable in here."

"I will be. *Denke* for having me here. I hope I'm not going to be too much trouble."

"You need to be with *familye* when the *boppli* comes. And after that too."

Anita sat on the bed.

"Dinner should be ready in an hour or so. Why don't you stay here and have a rest?" Hannah said.

"Denke, that would be nice. I am rather

tired even though I slept a great deal on the bus."

When Hannah walked out, Anita lay down on the bed, sank her head into the pillow, and then closed her eyes. This was the place her grandparents had lived when she and her brothers were growing up. Anita's parents had died before she and Joshua were married. Since Anita already had a house in Ohio, she let her brother take over the family home. Anita was the oldest, and only girl, and had four brothers younger than she. Amos was the youngest, and the only boy to stay in the Amish community.

Although Anita tried to have a sleep, she couldn't. There were so many memories connected to the house. There was still a faint smell of the tobacco her grandfather had smoked. Her grandmother never liked the smell and that was the only thing her grandmother and grandfather had ever argued about. Anita had to side with her grandmother especially now, with her unborn baby sharpening her sense of smell. Maybe with a new quilt, new curtains, and a fresh coat of paint, the smell would be gone.

"Are you hungry, Anita?"

Anita woke suddenly to see Hannah peering at her.

She realized she was at her brother's place and finally off the bus. She sat up. *"Jah,* I'm quite hungry." She was always hungry ever since the morning sickness had left her.

"I'm five minutes away from serving it."

"Denke, I'll get up and help."

"Nee, you stay and rest and I'll call you when it's ready."

When Hannah left her room, Anita stood up and stretched. Tomorrow she would open the doors and the windows to give the place a good airing out. She stepped into the bathroom and washed her face. When she looked into the mirror, she saw she had deep circles under her eyes. Anita wondered whether this was still the only mirror in the *haus.* It had been the only mirror many years ago. She'd had a mirror in her *haus* back in Ohio, but her parents had never liked mirrors in their *haus.* Her grandfather had put this one in, joking that it was so he and his wife could see how old they were getting.

She reached out for a towel, wiped her face, and then straightened her prayer *kapp.*

When Anita walked into the kitchen, she saw a young man sitting at the table with Amos.

Putting the last of the food on the table, Hannah said, "Anita, do you remember my *bruder* Simon?

"I think so. Hello, Simon."

"Nice to see you again, Anita."

Anita looked around for the boys, thinking how eager she was to play with them. Ben was sitting at a small table with an empty plate in front of him. Sam was nowhere to be seen. "Where's Sam?"

"Sam was cranky. He was overtired so we've put him to bed."

"Hannah, do you want me to put some food on Ben's plate?

"*Denke,* that would be good."

After she dished out some food for Ben, she sat at the table and waited for Hannah to sit down. When all the food was in the center of the table, everyone closed their eyes and gave a silent prayer of thanks for the food.

Anita looked at the spread of food and didn't know where to start. There were roasted vegetables and roasted chicken, coleslaw, mash potatoes, and a variety of other cooked vegetables. "This looks and smells *wunderbaar.*"

Hannah smiled. "Well help yourself. Here, give me your plate."

Anita passed her plate over and Hannah filled it, and then handed it back. "I don't think I can eat that much."

"You need to eat to keep your strength up. You're eating for two," Amos said gruffly.

Anita cut a piece of chicken, ready to pop it into her mouth when she felt Simon staring at her. She looked across at him.

"Sad to hear about your husband, Anita. Good news to hear about the *boppli.*"

He seemed a little awkward, as though he was genuinely sorry for her but struggled to find the appropriate words to express his feelings.

"Denke, Simon." Anita looked into Simon's face. He was handsome with his huge greenish-brown eyes and fresh face.

"Gott wanted Joshua back home. Nothing to be sad about," Amos said. "Life's a cycle – we live then we die. We don't know when *Gott's* going to call us home. No good going around all moony-faced feeling sorry for yourself."

Anita saw Amos suddenly flinch and

guessed that Hannah had kicked him under the table. Tears burned behind Anita's eyes. It was easy for Amos to say those things, but if he were a woman in her position with a baby on the way, would he be so dismissive of missing a spouse when he was gone forever? Anita was of the opinion that Joshua had been called home at the very worst possible time. Why couldn't Amos be a little more understanding?

Simon had raised his eyebrows at what Amos said and remained silent whereas, after Hannah had given Amos a good kick under the table, she sat staring down at her food.

To break the silence and change the mood, Anita said to Simon. "Do you live close by?"

"*Jah,* I do. I live right next door."

"At the Millers' old *haus?"*

Simon nodded. "I bought it from them a year ago."

"Simon took over *Dat's* business," Hannah said proudly.

"Your *vadder* made buggies, didn't he?"

Simon nodded. "That's right. I learned the trade from him, and now I've expanded to employ five men."

"That must keep you quite busy."

"It has been busy lately. Seems we've got no end of work."

Hannah turned toward Amos. "On the subject of work and keeping busy, I've been meaning to talk to you about something, Amos."

Amos finished swallowing the food in his mouth. "What is it?"

"I was wondering if you would mind if I worked two days a week in Libby's candy store."

Amos slowly placed his fork and knife down on his plate. "There's no need for you to work outside the home. You're always telling me how much you've got to do.

You've got enough to do inside this place. You're barely able to keep up with things around here. Why would you think to ask such a thing?"

"It's just that Libby asked me. She's been very busy and she's looking for someone to help her." Hannah pouted and looked down at her plate. "I thought it would be interesting, and it would get me out of the *haus.*"

"Why would you want to be out of the house?" Amos glared at Hannah.

Anita's heart was beating fast with the rising tension in the room. She glanced over at Simon wondering if he was feeling just as awkward as she. He raised his eyebrows when their eyes met.

"It was just an idea I had. Forget I mentioned it." Hannah shook her head.

"You haven't answered me. I asked why you'd want to be away from this *haus*. I work hard for you and the boys every day. You sound like you want a different kind of life."

"Amos, I don't think she said that she wants a different kind of life. Many women work a day or two out of the *haus.* Most every woman I know works a job a day or two a week," Simon said.

Amos turned to Simon. "That's because they need to bring money into the household. I provide well for my *fraa* and *kinner.* We have enough already. And it's really none of your concern, Simon."

Simon opened his mouth to reply, and Anita quickly said, "Is the meeting on this Sunday or the one after? I'm looking forward to seeing people I haven't seen in years."

The three people at the table stared at Anita.

Amos said, "The meeting is at the Fullers' this Sunday coming."

Anita put her hand to her forehead. *"Gut.* And what day is it today?"

"Today is Tuesday," Simon said

"Ben is being very quiet. He seems a good eater," Anita said trying to keep the conversation away from delicate subjects.

"*Jah,* he's a *gut* eater, just like his *Dat,*" Hannah said.

"I've noticed you've got bigger, Amos. You were tall and skinny when I left here."

"That was a long time ago, Anita. I've grown since you left."

"How long has it been since you've been here, Anita?" Simon asked.

"Since I left eight years ago to live with Joshua in Ohio."

"Joshua was your husband?"

Anita nodded.

"What's for dessert? I hope we've got more than just fruit again."

"We've got apple pie and cream," Hannah said looking pleased with herself.

"I love your apple pie," Simon said.

Amos said to Anita, "It's not as *gut* as *Mamm* used to make."

Hannah looked disappointed as she rose from the table to serve the dessert.

"I'll try it and let you know what I think, Hannah," Anita said.

"It's the best pie I've tasted," Simon said.

Anita swiveled around to face Hannah who was on the other side of the kitchen. "Do you need help?"

"Nee. I've everything ready."

When the dessert was over, Anita told Hannah that was the best pie she'd tasted. Hannah looked happy that she liked the apple pie.

"Simon and I will leave you ladies in here to wash up while we go to the living room."

"Nee, Anita should go to bed; she looks tired."

"I had a rest before. I feel fine."

"I'll help you with the dishes, Hannah," Simon said as he stood up.

Amos grumbled, "It's not men's work."

Simon turned to Amos, "It is if you're a

single man. I'll help with the dishes, and then I'll come into the living room."

Amos threw his hands in the air. "If that's what you want to do." Amos got up from the table, ordered Ben to pick up his plate and put it up at the sink. "He's ready for bed, Hannah."

While Hannah took Ben to bed, Amos went into the living room.

When Hannah came back to the kitchen, she said, "Please go and rest, Anita, you look awfully tired."

Anita knew she should look after herself and not push herself like she had been used to doing. "Okay *denke.* I will go to bed early since you've got someone to help you clean up."

Anita said goodnight to Hannah and Simon and walked to the end of the kitchen and slipped through the door to her *grossdaddi haus.*

She was too tired to wash, so she figured

she'd leave a shower until the morning. Anita took off her prayer *kapp* and shook out the braids from her long wavy dark hair. It fell to well below her waist. Since her brush was somewhere in the bag she hadn't unpacked, she simply ran her fingers through her hair to untangle it.

When she changed into her nightgown and got into bed, she was surprised how clearly she could hear them speak, since the kitchen and the *grossdaddi haus* shared a common wall.

She heard Simon say, "Why do you let him speak to you in that way?"

"What do you mean?" Hannah asked.

"You should stand up for yourself. I could tell you really want to work in that candy store."

"How could you tell that? I've never mentioned it to you."

Because I know you well. I could see the sparkle in your eyes when you spoke about it. And what would it hurt if you did that one or two days a week?"

Amos believes that he's the provider. I'm certain that he thinks if I work out of the *haus* people will think he's not being a *gut* provider."

"Aren't there scriptures about an industrious woman who works hard? I'm certain she worked in and out of the home. I think it's in Proverbs. You should remind him of that. No one said her husband wasn't providing enough."

"*Jah.* I remember reading that some time ago. I must find that passage, and read it again. Did you say it was in Proverbs?"

"I'm certain it is. You read it."

"I will."

"And then will you say something to him?"

"I might."

Anita heard Simon laugh. "*Nee* you won't. You're scared to say anything to him."

"Shh. He might hear you."

"I hope he does hear me! I might have a word with him myself."

"Don't you dare!"

That was all Anita overheard of their conversation before sleep overtook her.

CHAPTER 3

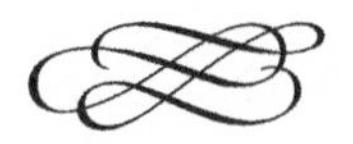

Yea, though I walk through the valley of the shadow of death, I will fear no evil: for thou art with me;
thy rod and thy staff they comfort me.
Psalm 23:4

Anita woke early and helped Hannah give the boys their breakfast.

When Amos came into the kitchen, they all sat at the table together.

"I've got to thinking, Anita," Amos said as he pushed egg onto his fork.

"Jah?"

"You're welcome to stay here forever, for as long as you want to, or as long as you need to."

Anita raised her eyebrows. They'd already had this conversation before she'd decided to move there. She kept quiet and waited for him to continue since he looked like he had something on his mind.

"Eventually, though, in time, you'll want to marry again."

Anita shook her head and placed her fork on her plate. "That's the last thing on my mind right now. I've just got to get this *boppli* into the world safely, and then I'll think about our future. Our future might include another man, and it might not. There's no rush for something like that." Anita stared at her insensitive brother and anger rose within her. "Why would you say something like this with Joshua not long gone? Can't you see what you're saying is upsetting?"

"*Jah,* Amos, I don't think she needs to worry about finding a man to take care of her right now. That's why she's here, so we can do that," Hannah said.

Amos ignored his wife and shook his head at Anita. "I think you're wrong. You shouldn't need people to take care of you when a man can do that. I'm not saying you're not welcome here. We'll always want you to stay in our home for as long as need be. I'm just saying you shouldn't wait too long before you marry again."

"Well, we'll see what happens." Anita picked up her fork and continued to eat.

He didn't stop there. "You need a new husband, and I'll help you find one."

Anita winced. "*Nee.*"

Hannah said, "Surely it's her decision, Amos. Joshua's not long been gone and she needs to be used to being without him."

Amos turned to look at his wife. "I think I know what's better for my own *schweschder* than you would."

"But would you know how a woman would feel? She's just said that she's not ready for anything like that. She can't be upset while she's expecting a child. And she needs some time for her heart to heal."

Amos shook his head. "I'm the head of this household, and I know best." He slapped a hand on the table and caused both women to jump.

Hannah looked over at Anita, and Anita managed to force a smile back at her. It was good of Hannah to come to her aid, but she didn't want to cause any trouble between the pair.

The sounds of a buggy approaching caused a hush of silence to sweep over the room.

"That'll be Simon coming to help me do work on the fences."

When Amos walked outside, Hannah said, "I'm so sorry, Anita. I had no idea that's what he had in his mind until he said it just now. I don't know why he didn't mention it to me before he said something to you. I would've made him see some sense."

Anita could see Hannah's bottom lip quivering slightly and she knew it'd taken a lot for her to say what she'd just said to Amos.

"Denke for what you said just now. I can see it might not be easy living with my *bruder,* he has such definite opinions on things."

Hannah gave a little giggle. "You noticed?"

Anita smiled and nodded. When Anita heard the two men talking outside, she stood up and looked out the kitchen window. She could see that Simon was the same height as her brother, and had a solid frame, but he was not overweight like her brother. "Why is your *bruder* helping Amos with the fences? Doesn't he have his own business, the buggy-making business?"

"When he's not there, he's got men working for him. Well he's really got men working for him all the time. He doesn't have to be there every day."

"Don't you mean to say that Amos asked him to help with the fences and Simon didn't like to say *nee?"* Anita tipped her head to the side waiting for Hannah to reply

Hannah giggled. "That's right. Simon likes helping him. Sometimes Amos helps him do things at his *haus."*

Sam accidently knocked over his breakfast bowl. Hannah went to rush over, but Anita said, "*Nee,* let me do it."

Sam started to cry.

"I'll get you some more." Anita wiped the egg off the floor. "You sit there and be a *gut bu* while I get you more, okay?"

Sam smiled. "Okay."

While Anita dished out some more eggs for Sam, and an extra helping for Ben, Hannah asked, "Would you like to come into town with me today, Anita? I need to get some supplies."

"I'd love to. Unless, you'd like to go by yourself? I could stay at home and mind the boys."

"Nee, I'd love you to come with me. I'll just have to wait for Amos to go, and then I'll hitch the buggy."

Anita crouched down and placed the two bowls on the small table in front of her young nephews. "There you go. Now eat up." When the two boys picked up their spoons and began to eat, Anita stood up. "Amos doesn't know you're going? Is that why you're waiting until he goes?"

"Nee, it's not that. I told him I was going out today. It's easier to hitch the buggy when he's not around because he doesn't like the

way I do it. He's always correcting me and telling me how to do it properly."

"I see. You're right, then, it'd be much better to do it when he's not around."

Hannah smiled brightly at her, and then plunged her hands into the sudsy dish-washing water. Anita picked up a clean dishtowel.

"The boys love going in the buggy," Hannah said.

"I guess they're at that age where they love everything. Everything is so new and exciting to them."

Hannah nodded. "You'll have one of your own to watch grow soon."

"I will, but I never thought I'd be doing it without Joshua."

"I know."

Anita was glad that Hannah didn't offer a multitude of reasons she shouldn't be sad about Joshua not being around.

"I don't know what I'd do if anything

happened to Amos." Hannah shook her head. "I don't even like to think about it." She passed a wet plate to Anita. "You must be a very strong person."

"I don't think of myself as strong, I've just got no choice but to carry on." Anita looked out the window at the vegetable garden. At this time of year, March, it was the best time to plant certain vegetables, especially cauliflower, and cabbage. Images of herself, as a girl, helping her grandmother plant vegetables in that very same patch of dirt, flashed through her mind. "What chores shall we do before we go out today?"

"None. Amos always takes the boys out every morning to collect the eggs, and to feed the chickens and pigs."

"He goes with the boys?"

"Jah." He likes to have time with them in the early hours before he goes out into the fields.

Anita was surprised because their father

had never gone with them when they were young. He'd shown them what to do once, and that was that. Even when Amos had been two years old, he'd had the job of collecting the eggs on his own. If he accidently dropped one on the way back to the house, he'd get into trouble, especially if the chickens hadn't laid many that day.

Hannah continued, "I'll do the washing tomorrow, and cook when we get home. There's nothing to do except get ready and go." Hannah frowned as she passed Anita another plate. "Are you up to it, or are you still tired?"

"I'm feeling good today, and I'm looking forward to seeing how the place has changed. It was too dark to see last night when we were coming here in the buggy."

"I guess there would be a few changes in the last eight years."

"Jah, I'm certain there would be."

"Where did the Millers' from next door move to?"

"They moved to a smaller *haus.* The farm was getting too much for them, and now that their boys have grown, they're working for other people. There was no sense to keep the farm."

Anita turned to look at the boys, and seeing they'd finished eating, she grabbed a cloth and wiped their faces and hands. Without being asked, Ben and Sam took their dishes to the sink.

"I'll go out and hitch the buggy," Hannah said.

"Do you want help?"

"Nee, but you could put the boys' coats on for me."

CHAPTER 4

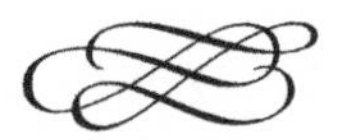

A new commandment I give unto you, That ye love one another; as I have loved you, that ye also love one another.
John 13:34

Just when they'd turned onto the road at the end of their driveway, Hannah said, "We'll be driving past Simon's *haus,* and you'll be able to see how much work he's done to it."

When the house came into view, Anita saw that Simon had extended the house. "It looks much bigger than I remember."

"He's added a main bedroom, and another bathroom, also an extra living room. And look at the barn." Hannah pulled the buggy off to the side of the road while they looked over at the barn.

"That's a lot of work. He's certainly done well for himself at such a young age. How old is he again?"

"He's twenty-two and he's been working for himself since he's been fifteen. He started off buying and selling horses and made a good sum doing that. He seems older than he is. He's much more mature than many of the other men his age."

"*Jah.* He does seem older from what I've seen of him. He'll make somebody a *gut* husband."

"I don't know if that will ever happen." Hannah clicked the horse forward.

Anita eyed Hannah carefully. "Why? What do you mean?"

"It's just that he doesn't seem to be interested in any of the girls in this community. Amos told him he should travel around the other communities to find a *fraa,* but Simon said that if it was meant to happen it would happen without him going out of his way. He's just been too fussy. He'll regret it when he's older. There are some girls in the community who like him, and he won't pay them any mind." Hannah pressed her lips together and shook her head.

"Perhaps he's not ready yet, or hasn't met the right girl?"

"Nee, he's just being fussy."

"He does have plenty of time."

Hannah looked over at her. "You know if you don't choose quickly, you run out of choices. What's he going to do, unless someone suddenly joins the community?"

"You mean like an *Englischer?"*

"Unless he goes and visits other communities, all he can do is wait until someone visits here, or hope that an *Englischer* will join us. That's a slim chance; how many *Englischers* join us? I suppose a few do, but what would be the chances that he'd like one of them?" Hannah looked over at Anita.

"That's how I met Joshua." Anita giggled. "I didn't mean he was an *Englischer,* of course, he wasn't. He was visiting this community when he came to work for his *onkel* for a few months."

Hannah glanced over at her again. *"Ach nee.* I didn't want to make you think about him. I should've been more careful what I talked about."

"It's okay for me to talk and think about him. It's not as though I can forget him, and I don't think I should." Anita looked down at her hands in her lap. When she looked back up at the road, she asked. "So where are we heading?"

"I need to get some groceries, and some fabric. I thought if we go to the farmers' markets, we can get everything there under the one roof."

"Perfect. I'll be glad to go there again. What do you need the fabric for?"

"I'm making your *boppli* a quilt."

Anita clapped her hands. "Are you? That's so lovely of you."

"You can help me choose the colors."

"That is exciting. I don't have anything for the *boppli* yet."

"I've got everything you could possibly need up until he or she is about twelve months old. And if he's a boy, he can always wear Sam and Ben's clothes that they've grown out of."

"Denke. That would be *wunderbaar.* That takes a lot of worry off me."

"I've got blankets, sheets, towels, everything you'll need."

When they pulled up in the parking lot of

the farmers' markets, Anita helped Hannah get the boys out of the buggy.

"They're old enough to walk everywhere, but they slow me down," Hannah explained. "When I've got a lot of shopping to do, I leave them with my *mudder* for a few hours."

"That's *gut* that you have your *mudder* to do things like that. I wish mine was still here." *Especially with my boppli coming soon.* Anita swallowed hard, and quickly added, "Is your friend's candy store around here somewhere?"

"It's just outside the markets. I'll take you there to have a look."

"Jah, I'd love to see it. I'm sure the boys would too."

Hannah frowned. "I don't let them eat candy. They're too young."

Anita shook her head. "I just thought they'd like to see all the bright colors."

"Let's go and get the fabric first." Hannah led the way.

When they walked into the store, Anita was overwhelmed with all the choices she had to make. There was the color, the pattern, the size. "I like the criss-cross pattern of that one. Is that something you could do?"

"*Jah,* I certainly think I could. And what colors?"

"Just some pale *boppli*-like colors – pinks, blues and yellow. Maybe with the main color cream?"

When they had made their selections, they headed out of the store. Hannah carried the bundle of fabric under her arm while holding onto Ben's hand, and Anita held onto Sam.

They stood outside the candy store and didn't go in because it was too crowded.

"Hannah, look at all these people."

"It gets busy like this when the tourist buses stop. It's not as busy as that all day, so Libby tells me."

"No wonder Libby needs an extra person

to help." Anita pressed her face closer to the window and shielded out the outside light with her hand so she could see inside better. "She's got three workers and they're all busy."

"It looks fun doesn't it?"

"I can see why you'd want to work there. It would certainly be lively."

When Anita turned around she expected to see Hannah, but jumped when she saw the bishop's wife, Fran standing where Hannah had been.

"I thought it was you, Anita. I was standing up there talking to someone and then I looked over and saw Hannah and the boys. John said you were coming back home. And I said I was glad you were. You don't want to be somewhere that isn't with *familye.* This is where you grew up and this is where you belong."

Anita smiled while Fran talked, and

glanced at Hannah who was standing behind Fran with a big grin on her face.

Fran glanced around at Hannah. "Where are you girls off to today?"

Hannah stepped closer. "We just had a few supplies to pick up. Anita just got here yesterday."

Fran smiled and patted Anita's stomach. "That's right, you're having a *boppli.* That's a blessing."

"Jah; it is a blessing."

"John's got a bad cold. He said he wanted to speak to you as soon as you got here; he's already told your *bruder* that, but I told him he's got to get rid of that nasty cold before we have you to the *haus.*"

Fran looked down at the boys, smiled at them, and then ruffled their hair. Ben smiled at her while Sam shied away. Fran chuckled at the boys and then looked up at Anita. "I'll see you on Sunday, if the Lord spares me."

Anita and Hannah watched Fran hurry away.

"She's like a tornado," Hannah said.

"Jah, she sure is. Doesn't stop to take a breath." Anita giggled. "I remember she always said, 'if *Gott* spares me' and when I was younger, I thought she was saying 'if *Gott* spears me.' I was wondering why she'd think *Gott* would spear her."

"I thought that same thing exactly when I was young."

Both girls laughed. Ben distracted them when he asked to go into the candy store.

"We'd better move away," Hannah said.

CHAPTER 5

Who knoweth not in all these that the hand of the LORD hath wrought this?

Job 12:9

When they arrived at the Fullers' *haus* for the Sunday meeting, Amos jumped out of the buggy first, and then got the boys out. Amos went off to talk to the men, while the two boys scrambled to hold Anita's hand.

"Seems I've fallen out of favor," Hannah said with a laugh.

"I've got two hands," Anita said to the boys. "One each." Each boy took hold of a hand, and then Anita and the boys followed Hannah into the house.

It was strange to be back. It seemed to Anita as though she'd stepped back in time. Hannah whispered to her that she liked to sit in the back with the boys in case they misbehaved and had to be taken outside.

"Anita."

Anita heard someone call her name and looked around to see Bishop John. "Hello."

He held her hand. "Amos told me you'd returned. I would've talked to you earlier but I had a nasty cold, and didn't want to pass it on since you're expecting."

Anita nodded. "*Jah,* I saw Fran a few days ago. You're feeling better now, I hope?"

"*Jah, jah.* Will you come by tomorrow? Fran and I would love to talk to you."

"I will. I'll look forward to it."

He patted her hand. "It's so *gut* to see you back here. Mid-afternoon would be the best time."

"I'll be there."

The bishop hurried away to talk to some other people.

"Come on, Anita. Let's go before all the back seats are taken."

The boys still had firm holds on Anita's hands. As she walked to the back, she smiled and nodded to people she recognized. She was pleased to see the friendly faces.

After some songs were sung, the deacon gave the word. He spoke on faith and how people need to trust *Gott* even though the outward appearances of situations might look bleak. He went on to say that *Gott* could see what we couldn't see of our future. The talk gave Anita encouragement.

When the meeting was over, the men moved the long wooden benches out of the house, and replaced them with tables for the meal. The women bustled around the kitchen and the annex outside the kitchen where the food was being prepared.

"They never had hot food after the meetings in my old community," Anita said to Hannah.

When Hannah didn't answer, Anita looked to see she was staring at something. Anita followed her gaze to see that she had her eyes fixed on a man who was walking toward them. He was an older man with dark hair and olive colored skin. Anita guessed him to be in his late forties. He was clean-shaven which meant he was a single man.

When he stood in front of them, Hannah said, "Anita, do you remember Hans Yoder?"

"*Jah,* I do." Anita remembered that Hans had been married and his wife had died.

Hans stood there staring at her, and when he opened his mouth to speak, another man came up to them. "Hello, Anita."

The man looked familiar, but Anita couldn't place who he was. She frowned. "Hello."

Hans stiffened, obviously put out by the interruption from the other man.

"Do you remember me?" the second man asked.

"Kind of, but…"

"I'm Billy."

"Billy, you've changed." 'Billy,' was Billy Miller, one of the Miller boys who used to live on the next-door farm. Billy was around three years younger than she.

Amos came up beside Anita and took hold of her arm. "If everyone will excuse us, I need to borrow Anita for a minute." Without waiting for any kind of reply. Amos pulled Anita away.

"What are you doing, Amos? That was a bit rude."

"Humph. Billy's too young for you, and you don't want someone ancient like Hans.

It's ridiculous; he's old enough to be your *vadder.* I don't know what he's thinking."

"They were just being friendly."

He shook his head. "*Nee.* Trust me, they weren't. "

Anita stopped still and stamped her foot. "I'm having a baby and I'm recently widowed, Amos. You're acting like I'm a prime piece of meat that the crows are circling, and I'm not!"

"Maybe not back in Ohio, but here, a prime piece of meat is exactly what you are. You're an attractive woman, Anita, and you'll give a man a head start to a *familye.*"

Anita shook her head. She knew she wasn't pretty, not at all. She was plain, and that's just how she liked it.

"Now come on." Amos grabbed her arm again, and continued walking.

Anita looked up and saw her brother was taking her toward Mark Yoder, Hans' younger brother.

She remembered Mark from school, and she knew he was the same age as she was. What's more, she knew that Mark had always liked her. He'd asked her on a buggy ride once, but Anita had refused him because she had just met Joshua.

When they stood in front of him, Mark said, "Nice to see you again, Anita. I thought it was you when I saw you just now in the *haus.*"

Anita nodded, and swallowed hard. He had grown more handsome with age. Before she could answer, Amos said, "I have to see someone about something." Amos walked away.

Anita tried to hide her annoyance with her brother so she wouldn't be rude to Mark. "Hello, Mark. How have you been?"

"I've been *gut.* I heard that your husband has gone to be with *Gott.*"

"*Jah,* he has."

Anita noticed his eyes glance at her belly,

but he didn't mention the baby she was carrying. She had no idea what to say to him, and when he didn't speak, she could only think to ask about the buggy he was leaning against. "This your buggy?"

"*Jah,* it is. I've just got a new horse." He turned and patted the shiny black horse on his rump.

Anita stepped closer to look at the horse. "Looks nice." She wondered why Mark wasn't married. He seemed nice enough and he was twenty-eight, the same age as she was. It was old for a man in the community to still be unmarried.

"I better go back and see if Hannah needs my help with her *kinner.*"

"Wait!"

She looked up at him.

"Would you like to spend some time with me?"

Anita's heart raced and she could feel her cheeks burn. She'd have a stern talk with

Amos and tell him not to try to match her with anyone. Anita shook her head. "*Nee*. It's too soon after Joshua..."

"Life goes on."

"*Jah*, it certainly does." Anita turned and walked away. That was just it. She didn't want life to go on. It seemed strange that the world continued just the same as it always had right after Joshua had gone. She wanted the world to stop and acknowledge that her Joshua was no longer amongst the living, but the world and the people in it carried on regardless.

Anita headed straight to Hannah who seemed the safest person to stay around. Before she reached her, Amos cut her off.

Anita held up her hands. "Don't say anything. Please, just don't!" She walked past him and found Hannah. She stayed with Hannah, helping with the boys until it was time to go home.

CHAPTER 6

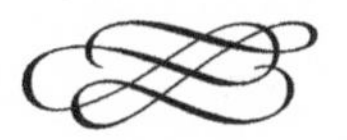

While the earth remaineth, seedtime and harvest,
and cold and heat, and summer and winter,
and day and night shall not cease.
Genesis 8:22

Anita was pleased to take the buggy by herself the next day and head to he bishop's *haus.* She always felt a sense of peace when she drove the buggy down the narrow winding roads to Fran and Bishop John's house.

When she was tying the reins of the buggy to the post, Fran rushed out toward her.

"Come in, Anita. It's so *gut* to have you here. Come into the *haus.*" When Anita was seated in the living room, Fran said, "John will be out in a minute."

Anita looked around the room. It hadn't changed since the last time she'd been there, and she was sure the last time she'd been there was with Joshua just before their wedding.

"You wait here and I'll bring out the tea."

Anita was sitting on one of the two couches in the room. The bishop came out, and sat on the couch opposite just as Fran came back with a large tray. Fran placed the tray on the table between the couches.

"How do you have your tea, Anita?" Fran said.

"I'll have it black, *denke.*" Anita normally didn't drink tea at all, but it looked like Fran had gone to a lot of trouble to make it.

"Black? I don't know how you could like it black." After Fran passed her a teacup and saucer, she cut into the chocolate cake. All the while John remained quiet while Fran fussed about.

"That cake looks *wunderbaar,*" Anita said.

"I hope so." She cut a large piece, and placed it on the coffee table near Anita.

When she passed her husband a cup, she sat next to him and folded her hands neatly in her lap.

The bishop turned to his wife, *"Denke,* Fran."

She smiled at him.

The bishop looked over at Anita and when he opened his mouth to speak, his wife said, "So lovely to hear you're having a *boppli.*"

"*Jah,* it is. And it's *gut* to have you back here," the bishop said.

Anita nodded and took a sip of tea, pretending she liked the taste. It wasn't too bad, it was fairly weak so was just like sipping on hot water.

"What are your plans?" the bishop asked.

Anita took a deep breath. She hadn't really made plans for herself, she was too weak to think and had just gone along with whatever Amos had suggested. "When Joshua went to be with *Gott,* Amos insisted I come back here and live with him. I leased out my house, and came back here. It seemed like the best thing to do. Amos is the only *familye* I have now that all my other brothers have left the community."

"We're all your *familye,*" the bishop's wife said.

Anita smiled at her.

The bishop asked, "You're going to stay on, then, after the *boppli* arrives?"

"I guess so." Anita's eyes were drawn to the cake; it looked too good to resist. Anita dug the fork in , broke off a portion, and placed it into her mouth. It was moist and the chocolate flavor was strong.

Just then, someone knocked on the door and Fran got up to answer it.

"Do you think it's a *gut* idea for me to stay?" Anita asked the bishop when she'd swallowed.

The bishop nodded. "*Jah,* I do."

Fran came back wringing her hands. "It's Lydia son, Paul. Lydia's sick again and wants prayer."

The bishop jumped to his feet. "Anita, we'll have to cut the visit short."

Anita pushed herself to her feet. "Of course."

"*Nee,* you stay, Anita," Fran insisted.

The bishop glanced at his wife and then said, "*Jah,* sure, stay and talk to Fran."

Anita sat, pleased she'd be able to finish

off the chocolate cake and perhaps get the recipe. She wasted no time sticking her fork into the cake again for another mouthful. When she'd swallowed, she asked, "Is that Lydia Hostetler who's ill?"

"*Jah*, she's not been too good."

Anita remembered Lydia; she'd been an elderly woman back before Anita had left for Ohio. "She'd be quite old now, wouldn't she?"

"She's nearly ninety."

Anita nodded, and thought she should take another sip of tea. "Are you having cake?" she asked Fran.

"I've already had some today."

"It's delicious. Do you think I might be able to have the recipe?"

"*Jah*. It's made with real chocolate, not just the powdered cocoa. It's a bother to make, but it's worth it."

"Well, I hope Mrs. Hostetler feels better."

"Now, let's talk about you."

Anita looked over at Fran to see her staring intently at her.

"What about me?" Anita gave a little laugh.

Fran stood up. "I've written out a list for you. I'll go and get it."

Anita filled her mouth with more chocolate cake while she waited. When Fran returned, she took a sip of tea, and then took the piece of paper from her.

"It's a list of names," Fran said.

"Oh *wunderbaar.* That's so thoughtful of you. I haven't even given any thought to names." Anita looked down the list, and then looked up at Fran. "What if it's a girl? Have you a list of girls' names?"

Fran giggled, and put her hands up to her face. "*Nee,* Anita. This is a list of suitable *menner* in the community for you."

Anita gulped.

"They're all single, or widowed. I've underlined all the widowers and not all of them are old."

Anita looked down at the list again. She'd thought they were baby names. "There certainly are a lot of them."

"*Jah.* There are a lot to choose from. Women are scarce, men are plentiful, so *gut* for you."

While Anita wondered if she should inform Fran that finding another man was the last thing on her mind, she took a sip of tea, which had turned lukewarm. She set the tea back down on the table in front of her. Somehow she didn't like to disappoint Fran by telling her how she truly felt. "It was very nice of you to go to all this trouble, Fran." She would much rather the cake recipe had been written. She knew it was no use explaining how she felt to people who'd never been in the same situation.

"We don't want the devil to get a foothold, do we?"

"A foothold?"

"Let every man have his own wife, and every woman her own husband."

Anita knew the quote was from Corinthians. Fran clearly thought everyone should marry so they weren't tempted by sins of the flesh.

Anita patted her stomach. "I think I've got a distraction from all of that."

"It's not going to be *gut* if you stay in your *bruder's haus* forever. I'm sure you'll feel you're a burden on them before long."

Anita didn't like having to rely on anyone. She didn't tell Fran she already felt like an intruder in her brother's life. "It won't be forever."

"And neither should it be. Not when there are so many men who could give you and the *boppli* a home."

"Denke so much for the visit. I think I need to go now. I'm suddenly feeling a little tired." Anita stood up, and Fran stood too.

"Take this with you." Fran picked up the list of bachelors and widowers, took hold of Anita's hand, and closed her fingers over it.

"Denke." Anita couldn't leave the house fast enough. She threw the list on the buggy seat next to her, took hold of the reins and clicked the horse forward. She looked back to see Fran standing outside the house waving, looking pleased with herself.

CHAPTER 7

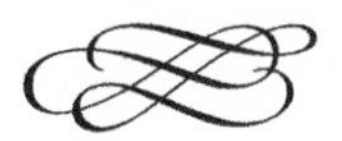

And be not conformed to this world: but be ye transformed by the renewing of your mind, that ye may prove what is that good, and acceptable, and perfect, will of God.
Romans 12:2

When she was nearly back at the house, she saw a wagon by the roadside. She looked closer and saw that Simon was nearby. She pulled up the buggy behind his wagon.

He turned to see her and waved. "Hello."

She got down from the buggy and walked toward him. "What are you doing out this way?"

"Mending some of my fences."

"This is your land too?"

"Jah, I bought this land before I bought the *haus.* It joins mine. The land where the old Millers' *haus* is."

When she got even closer, she noticed his hand was bleeding. "What happened?"

"I was careless. Some wire sprang back and cut me."

"That's awful. Give me a look."

He held his hand back. "It's not that bad." She stepped closer to take his hand, and he stepped away further. "Don't get any on your white apron."

"Hold it out and show me, then."

"Bossy like your *bruder,* are you?" He smiled as he held his hand out.

She looked into his eyes. "No one could be as bossy as that." They both laughed. She took hold of the part of his hand that wasn't bleeding. "It looks deep; you'll have to put something on it."

"Okay, if you think so."

"Come back with me to Amos' *haus* and I'll fix it for you."

"Nee, I'm not exactly a person he wants to see right now."

Anita frowned and wondered why, but didn't ask. She didn't want to be drawn into any disagreements.

"My place is closer," he said.

"Okay. I'll follow you there. Are you all right to drive the wagon?"

"I only need one hand." He held up his good hand.

When they reached Simon's *haus,* Anita stepped down from the buggy. "We'll need some iodine, and a bandage or some clean rags."

"I've got all that in the kitchen."

He opened the door and she followed him through to his kitchen. She held his hand over the sink as she cleaned the wound the best she could. Then she poured iodine over it.

"I don't think you'll need stitches," she said.

"Not if you bind it tightly. The body heals itself."

She wound a bandage around his hand as firmly as she could while being careful not to bind it too tightly.

"You've done this kind of thing before?"

She smiled and nodded. "Joshua always found ways to cut and injure himself." She ripped the end of the bandage and tied it together. "There, all done."

"*Denke*. Now, I should offer you something. *Kaffe?*"

Coffee sounded great. "*Jah,* please! You sit, Simon, I'll get it."

"*Nee,* I can do it. I only need one hand. You sit." He laughed.

She pulled a seat out from under the kitchen table and sat down wondering what Fran would say if she saw her in a bachelor's house straight after her warning about the devil getting a foothold. "I've just been to visit the bishop."

He looked over his shoulder, from filling up the pot with water. "How did that go?"

"He was called away because Lydia Hostetler needed prayer."

"*Jah,* she's not been too good for some time." He placed the pot on the stove and fetched two mugs.

"Are you sure you can do it by yourself."

"*Jah.* You didn't happen to have any of Fran's chocolate cake did you?"

"Isn't that the best? It's the finest cake I've ever tasted. She said she'd give me the recipe, but I left in a hurry and forgot to get it."

He sat down at the table with her. "She really said she'd give it to you?"

"*Jah*. Why?"

"She never gives out her recipes. You shouldn't have left without it."

Anita gave a little giggle. "I don't normally like cake, but her chocolate cake is so moist. She said she makes it with real chocolate."

"Ah, I'll have to try that next time," Simon said.

"You bake?"

"I've been known to."

"You live on your own, so I guess you cook for yourself?"

"I am over at my *schweschder's* place a lot, if you hadn't noticed."

"I have." Anita smiled. She always had reason to smile when Simon was around. He had such a relaxed nature.

Simon got up to pour the coffee. "How do you have it?"

"I have it black."

"Me too, but only because I'm always running out of milk."

He placed a coffee mug on the table in front of her. She brought it to her lips and took a sip. "Mmm, that's nice."

He took a sip too. "I should offer you something to eat." He sprang to his feet.

"*Nee,* I'm fine. I've just had chocolate cake."

He sat back down.

"You're not at work today?" Anita asked.

"It's a public holiday today, which means I've got to give my workers a day off, or pay them an obscene amount of money. They're happy to take a day off. Now that I've got *Englischers* working for me I have to take notice of things like holidays and the like."

"*Jah,* I suppose you would."

"How are you settling in?"

"Everything's going fine." Anita looked away from him and stared down into her coffee. "It's just different from what I thought things would be like."

"I guess you never expected to be in the situation you're in now."

Anita nodded. "Exactly. Amos has been good to me, and Hannah is lovely. The two boys are precious. It'll be good for my child to grow up with them and they'll be like siblings."

Simon had a mouthful of coffee.

Anita saw some blood coming through his bandage. "Oh, look!"

He looked down at it, and said, "It'll be okay. I'm tough."

"Maybe you should go and get it looked at."

"I might later. I'll see how it goes." He looked at her face and laughed. "Don't worry. I suppose you miss your friends?"

"I miss them terribly. I'll write to them

and call them, but it's not the same as seeing them."

"It'll take a while for you to make a life here, but everything will come right for you in time."

"It will?" He seemed to be so confident and self-assured. Anita wished she had his confidence that the future would be bright.

"I know it will."

After ten more minutes talking to Simon, she was certain she'd found a friend. He was kind, intelligent, and funny. "I guess someone will be wondering where I've gotten to."

"Someone whose name is Amos?"

Anita giggled and rose to her feet. "Do you need help with anything before I go? You can't do too much with that hand of yours."

"I'll be fine. Come on, I'll walk you out."

When they were close to the buggy, a gust of wind blew Fran's list off the buggy seat and it flew into the air. Simon jumped up and caught it. "What's this?" He looked down at the list of names, and then back at her.

Anita put her hand over her mouth to stifle her laughter. "Fran gave me a list of names and I thought they were suggestions for baby names. Turns out, they were names of men for me to consider."

Simon raised his eyebrows. "For marriage?"

Anita nodded.

Simon's eyes grew wide as he smiled. "Really?" He took another look at the list. "My name's not on here. I'll have to have a word with Fran."

Anita laughed. "Well don't tell her you've seen the list. It might be a secret list, or something."

"Maybe she wants you to close your eyes and stick a pin into the list and marry the man whose name you stick with the pin."

They both laughed.

Suddenly Simon stopped laughing as he looked at something by the road. Anita turned to see what he was looking at. It was Amos driving toward his house.

"Here's trouble," Simon said.

"I'd better go." Anita climbed into the buggy. She'd only just turned the buggy around, when Amos drew level. Anita could tell by his eyes that he was fuming.

"Home now, Anita," Amos yelled.

"Simon hurt his hand," she said.

"I said, *now!*"

Anita drove the horse forward and traveled the small distance to Amos' house. She wondered what the two men would say to each other.

When she got home, she told Hannah what had happened so Hannah would know to expect Amos to come home in a bad mood.

"Should I take Ben and Sam outside when he comes home?" Hannah asked.

"It might be a *gut* idea. I think he was fairly angry with me." Anita heard his buggy. "Sounds like that's him now."

Hannah ushered the boys outside.

Anita sat in the living room and waited for him to come inside. She considered it would be a good sign if he unhitched the buggy first before he came in. If he were really mad, he'd leave the buggy and come straight in to talk to her. She heard his footsteps pounding toward the house and knew he was thoroughly upset with her.

He took off his boots at the door, and when he stepped through, Anita watched him hang his hat on the peg behind the door. He walked over and sat in front of her. "What were you doing at Simon's *haus;* alone with him?"

"I told you. He cut his hand and I was helping him."

"Why not bring him here?"

Anita couldn't tell him it was because of

his objectionable personality that Simon didn't want to come there. "His home was closer."

"Our place is only next door to his; only another two minutes by buggy."

She had no answer so looked down. *Why did people always think the worst of situations?*

"He's no good for you, Anita. And, I'm surprised at you."

Anita shook her head. "There's nothing to be surprised about. I was just helping him with his hand. Didn't he tell you that? Or didn't you let him speak?"

"I talked to him."

Talked 'at him' more like it. "Anyway, what's wrong with him?"

"If you hadn't noticed, he's far too young for you. He's a bad choice."

Anita giggled at the silliness of the situation and at her brother's worried face.

He shook his head at her. "I'm only trying to look after you, Anita."

Anita stopped laughing when she saw the sincerity in his eyes. *"Denke,* Amos. You are looking after me, and looking after me very well. The thing you have to know is that I'm not a sixteen-year-old girl and you're not my *vadder."*

His lips twitched at the corners and Anita saw that as his way of smiling. Anita pushed herself up from the couch. "Now stop worrying about me little *bruder.* I'm not interested in any man. I'm just concerning myself with my *boppli."*

Amos stood up and all six foot four of him loomed over her. "I'll try and remember that."

"See that you do."

"I better go and tend to the horse."

Anita nodded. When he left the house, Anita went into the garden to find Hannah and tell her that they'd resolved their problem – for now.

CHAPTER 8

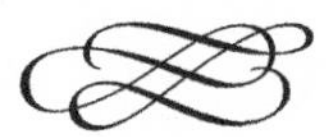

And God shall wipe away all tears from their eyes; and there shall be no more death, neither sorrow, nor crying, neither shall there be any more pain: for the former things are passed away.
Revelation 21:4

As Anita was setting the dinner table for dinner, Hannah said, "Simon always comes over for dinner every second night."

"Okay." Anita knew he was there a lot, but didn't realize it was as often as every second night. She set an extra place for him.

When the evening meal was ready, Hannah said, "I wonder what's keeping Simon. He's not usually late."

"He's not coming tonight."

Both women turned around to see Amos in the doorway of the kitchen.

"Why's that? Is he unwell?" Hannah asked.

"His hand's not worse, is it?" Anita asked.

Amos raised his hands. "He wasn't able to make it tonight."

"When did he tell you that?" Hannah asked.

"I saw him earlier today. I didn't think to tell you because you always cook too much food. One less mouth at the table wouldn't have made a difference."

Anita and Hannah looked at each other. Anita knew she and Hannah were thinking the very same thing. Amos had told Simon not to come for dinner.

Dinner was eaten quietly that night with the only noises coming from Ben and Sam. Anita wanted to make conversation but couldn't think what to talk about. She was glad when dinner was over and Amos was out of the room. She cleared the plates off the table while Hannah put the children to bed.

"I thought they were friends," Anita whispered when Hannah had returned to the kitchen.

"He's overprotective of you, that's all. He'll calm down."

Anita felt bad that the two men were at odds just because she was staying at the house. "Well, he's got no need to be overprotective of me; I'm a grown woman capable of looking after myself and making my own decisions."

"He doesn't like anyone to make the decisions around here. He likes to be the only one with any say."

"You thinking about your friend's candy store?"

Hannah nodded. "I'd like to get out of the *haus.* It would also be *gut* to have a little money that's just my own."

"Did you ask him again?"

She shook her head. "It would make him mad if I asked again. He'd say I wasn't respecting him."

"He'll come around in time."

"Nee, he won't."

"Do you want me to say something?"

Hannah turned to Anita with her face beaming. "Would you?"

Anita had expected Hannah to say 'no.' "Okay." Now that she'd offered she'd have to speak to him. "I'll take a cup of tea out to him and bring up the subject."

"Denke. I'll put the pot on to boil."

Anita wasn't looking forward to speaking to her brother about a delicate subject for the second time in one day, but there was no going back. When the tea was made, Anita breathed in deeply, and ventured into the living room.

"Can I talk to you about something?" she asked.

He closed his bible and placed it on the table beside his chair. "All right. I told him not to come around here anymore." He held up his hand. "And before you say anything about fixing his hand, I can tell you I see the way he looks at you."

Anita passed him the tea and sat on the couch next to him. "Actually, *bruder* dear, I was going to speak to you about something very different."

He remained quiet and rubbed his beard. Anita didn't think that Simon had looked at her in a peculiar way at all. Surely Simon didn't see her as anything other than a relative by marriage, perhaps someone he got along with, but definitely not a marriage prospect.

Amos took a slurp of tea. "What was it you wanted to speak to me about?"

"It's about Hannah."

He narrowed his eyes as though he suspected they'd been conspiring against him. Anita quickly added, "What harm would it do to let her work at her friend's store one or two days a week?"

He breathed out heavily. "Is that something she really wants to do?"

Anita nodded. "She'd really like it."

He bit his lip and looked down. "I suppose you think I'm an unreasonable man."

"*Nee,* I don't. You're a *gut* man. Very *gut,* and a *wunderbaar bruder.*"

He chuckled. "If it doesn't interfere with things she has to do around here, I don't suppose it would hurt. She'd have to get her *mudder* to mind the *kinner.*"

"I'm sure her *mudder* would love to do that."

Amos yelled out, "Did you hear that, Hannah? I said you could give it a try."

Hannah raced into the room. *"Denke."* She rubbed Amos on his shoulder.

Anita thought it best to leave the two of them alone. "I'll make an early night of it."

"Do you want me to bring you something, Anita?" Hannah asked.

Anita pushed herself off the couch. *"Nee,* I'm fine."

When Anita closed the door behind her, she was pleased to have a little space she could call her own. It wasn't the big home she owned in Ohio, but it was somewhere she could shut everyone out and have privacy. Amos wasn't so bad, he was just trying to do the best he could for everyone. *He could be feeling a heavy burden having a familye and a schweschder to look after.*

After she had a shower, she sat on the bed and brushed her hair while wondering about what Amos had said. He said he'd seen the way Simon had looked at her. Had she ever seen Simon look at her as though he liked her? She closed her eyes and recalled all the times she'd seen Simon. All she could recall was his smiling face. Maybe that's what Amos had seen. She braided her hair so it wouldn't tangle in her sleep, and then threw the brush on the bed.

When she walked over to turn the lamp off, she caught a glimpse of the moon out the window. She put her elbows on the windowsill and stared up at it. *Where are you Joshua? I'd give anything to see you just one more time. All I have are memories.* She patted her belly. *And our boppli.*

Anita closed the window, and hoped that her coming there wouldn't cause a rift between Amos and Simon.

CHAPTER 9

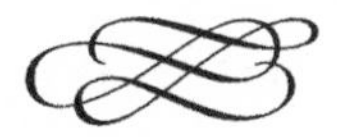

And let us not be weary in well doing: for in due season we shall reap, if we faint not.
Galatians 6:9

A few days later, Anita was in the kitchen after breakfast and caught sight of a buggy coming towards the house. "Who's that, do you think?" she asked Hannah.

Hannah rushed to her side and looked out the window. "That's Mark Yoder."

Mark Yoder was the man her brother thought would make her the best match.

"Why is he coming by? Did Amos invite him?" Anita stared at Hannah and Hannah looked away.

"Help me out here, Hannah. I helped you with getting a couple days at the candy store."

Hannah smiled. "Amos thinks that the pair of you would be a good match."

"That's the last thing on my mind right now the last thing – the absolute last thing."

"Maybe it's the last thing on your mind, but it might be something that would be good for you. Did you think of that?"

Anita raised her eyebrows. *"Nee.* I never considered that it might be a good thing for me when it's the *last* thing that I want."

"We can't turn him away now that he's

here." She placed her hands on Anita's shoulders to face her directly. "Now let me have a look at you." Hannah pushed some of Anita's hair back under her prayer *kapp.* "Your hair is always sliding out of your *kapp.*"

"Stop it!" Anita slapped Hannah's hands away causing Hannah to laugh. "I'm not the slightest bit interested. I don't want to waste his time and I don't want to waste my time. How can we make his visit the shortest possible?" She looked at Hannah who didn't look concerned. "Come on, Hannah, help me. You don't know how awful this is for me."

"You could say you don't feel well and need to go lie down. That would be understandable in your condition."

"Great idea. *Denke.* That's exactly what I'll do."

As the ladies went out to meet Mark, he pulled up the buggy in front of the house.

Anita could see that Mark had a wide grin on his face.

Hannah said, "This is an unexpected surprise. Does Amos know you were coming here?"

"I saw Amos up the road. He said to come here and he'd be here soon. I need to talk to him about a matter. I'll just wait for him in the buggy." He nodded hello to Anita and she nodded back.

"Nonsense. Come into the *haus* and I'll make you a cup of *kaffe*. Anita has just baked chocolate cake. You can be the first to taste it."

"Denke. I won't deny myself a slice of chocolate cake," Mark said as he jumped down from the buggy.

Mark strode off toward the house and Anita glared at Hannah. Hannah hadn't tried too hard to get rid of the man. Anita had to wonder whether Hannah was willingly in the conspiracy with Amos.

The pot had been on the boil before Mark had showed up. Just as the three of them were in the house, they heard Amos' buggy.

"Here he is," Hannah said.

"You sit down with Mark, Hannah, I'll make the *kaffe.*"

Before Hannah could say anything, Anita had given Hannah a shove toward the living room, and then Anita slipped into the kitchen. While she was making the coffee, she heard her brother come into the house. It wasn't long after that he poked his head into the kitchen.

"Why aren't you with our guest?" Amos asked Anita.

"Someone has to make the *kaffe* and get everything ready. Hannah works so hard all the time. I'm just giving her a rest while the *kinner* are having their sleeps." It would do no good to tell Amos again that she wasn't interested in Mark or anyone else. He hadn't heard her the first time, so the best thing she could think of was to excuse herself early just as Hannah had suggested.

Anita looked up at her brother to see him staring at her. Knowing he was about to say something, she got in before him, and said, "Go on. You go out and talk to him; I'll be out in a minute."

When her brother walked out, Anita arranged the cake and the coffee cups on the serving tray. Every minute she was in the kitchen was one less minute she'd have to spend in Mark's company.

When Anita carried the tray into the room, Mark bounded to his feet to take it from her. "Let me help you with that. You shouldn't be carrying heavy things."

"Denke." Anita sat down on the couch while Mark turned to place the tray on the table in between the two couches. Anita had nowhere to sit but on the same couch where

Mark had just been sitting, and he sat beside her after he'd set down the tray.

The conversation, steered by Amos, quickly turned to what a good cook Anita was. She knew that the chocolate cake in front of them wasn't very good. Anita had been trying out a few recipe variations, hoping to replicate Fran's chocolate cake. None of the cakes she'd made so far had come anywhere near Fran's. Over the past days she'd considered simply asking Fran for the recipe, but feared Fran might have asked her how she was getting on with that list of names.

Anita wanted to laugh out loud at how ridiculous the situation was with everyone praising her cooking while eating the dismal chocolate cake.

Anita stood. "If everyone will excuse me, I feel I just need to lie down for a little while."

Mark placed his coffee cup onto the table. "Are you okay, Anita?"

"I'm fine. I'm just a little tired, that's all." Anita put a hand to her head, turned around and walked out the room. She walked into her *grossdaddi haus,* closed the door behind her, and then collapsed onto the bed.

Anita felt as though she were a teenager and her parents were trying to force her to marry a man. And just like a teenager, she was tempted to escape out the window. She glanced at the door of the *grossdaddi haus* that led outside. She wondered when Simon might be coming to dinner again. She felt comfortable with him and she could talk with him like a good friend. Anita closed her eyes and figured she might as well have a real rest.

A few minutes later, Hannah knocked on her door, and then opened it slightly. Anita looked over to see that Hannah had poked her head through the doorway.

"He's gone," she said. "You can come out now."

Anita smiled, pleased to have Hannah on her side. "Thanks for letting me know."

"Amos has gone too."

"Even better." Anita was relieved that she would avoid confrontation with her brother about being rude to the man who had come to visit her. It was surely no secret that Mark had come to see her. What other reason had he for dropping by?

"Is Amos angry with me?" Anita asked.

"Nee. Why would he be, if you're tired and needed to have a lie down?" The corners of Hannah's lips turned upwards.

"Denke for saving me from an awkward time."

"Well, I did owe you one."

"Jah, and speaking of that when do you start?"

"I start next week."

"What day?"

"I'm to work Tuesdays and Thursdays."

"Do you want me to look after the boys for you?"

"Nee. That's kind of you to offer, but my *mudder* is happy to look after them."

Anita stretched her hands over her head, and yawned. "I'll be out in a minute."

After Hannah closed the door, Anita wondered what she'd do on the days when Hannah was working. She'd miss her and the boys on those days. At that moment she was glad that she wasn't living all alone back in the house she'd lived in with Joshua. Maybe Amos had been right when he'd insisted she'd be better off living with him.

After Anita splashed cold water on her face, she went into the kitchen to help Hannah with the chores. She saw that the boys were now awake and Hannah was feeding the little one on her lap.

Anita sat next to her.

"When is your appointment with the midwife?" Hannah asked.

"That's on Tuesday." Anita realized that was the same day that Hannah would be working.

"Well you take the buggy on that day, and I'll have Libby pick me up and drop me home. Amos can take the boys to my *mudder's.*"

"Denke, but do you think you should ask Amos to do that? I don't know if he'd like it that your job was giving him something extra to do, especially on your first day."

"You're right. I'll tell you what, I don't think Libby would mind if she takes me to drop the boys off on the way."

"Are you sure?"

"It's on the way, and it's only for one day. Other days I can drive the buggy myself."

"That sounds *gut.* And I'll make sure I don't make appointments on Tuesdays or Thursdays."

Anita was pleased at the thought of having her independence on Tuesday. If she had the buggy for the whole day, she could come and go as she pleased without anyone watching over her shoulder.

"I might have to warn you of something," Hannah said.

"What now? Warn me of what?" Anita grimaced.

"Amos has it in his head that you should marry again and I don't think he's going to let that idea go."

Anita sighed. As soon as Hannah had said she had something to warn her about, she immediately knew it had something to do with Amos. "Who knows? One day I might marry again, but right now, it's the furthest thing from my mind and the last thing that I want. Nothing Amos does or says can change that."

Hannah spooned food into Sam's mouth, and then looked across at Anita and smiled.

"*Denke,* for the warning anyway, Hannah. Now, what shall we do with the rest of the day?"

"I need to do washing, but that'll have to wait until tomorrow. It's too late in the day for it to dry now. I've got the dinner started for tonight as well. There's not much for us to do."

Anita knew that Amos looked after the animals; the pigs, chickens, and the horses. "If you've already got the dinner going, why don't we pull some weeds? The boys can play outside while we do it."

"*Jah.* I've been thinking that we need to weed around the vegetables. I haven't done that in some time. I'm glad Amos hasn't noticed. He hardly ever goes out into the back garden."

"It must be hard to get things done, with two boys to watch."

"One was much easier, but two seems more than double the work. I don't know how people with ten or twelve *kinner* do everything."

"The older ones help the younger ones. That's the only way."

CHAPTER 10

And he said unto me, My grace is sufficient for thee:
for my strength is made perfect in weakness.
Most gladly therefore will I rather glory in my infirmities,
that the power of Christ may rest upon me.
2 Corinthians 12:9

When Tuesday came, Anita helped get the boys ready for their day with their grandmother. She walked them outside and waited for Libby to collect them and their mother.

Hannah turned to Anita. "*Ach, nee.* I haven't hitched the buggy for you to go to the midwife."

"I'll be able to do it myself. I'm not that far gone. Besides, many women have to do things like that for themselves when they're much further along than this." She put her hands on her belly.

"Are you certain? I could find Amos on the farm and ask him to do it. I'm certain he said he's riding the boundary fences today."

Anita shook her head. "Don't concern yourself with me. You go and sell a lot of candy, or make it, or whatever you'll be doing there."

Hannah's face beamed. "I'll be selling it. That means I'll be seeing so many people and talking to them."

They both turned when they heard a buggy, looking down to the end of the long driveway.

"Here she is now."

Anita leaned down and kissed the boys goodbye. Ben threw his arms around her neck and kissed her on the cheek.

Once they were all in the buggy, Libby turned it around, and Anita watched them leave until the buggy met the road at the end of the driveway.

It felt odd to be on her own. She thought she'd feel free, but the lack of people around just made her feel sorry for herself.

She was happy that Hannah was getting to do what she wanted and she wondered whether Amos would've let Hannah do that if she hadn't spoken to him. Perhaps she was making a difference in their lives for the better. Is that why she was here?

She went inside and tidied up the house in the hour she had before she had to leave to see the midwife. Anita finished washing the morning dishes, she scrubbed the kitchen, and then washed the kitchen floor. When the time came, she swung on her black cape, placed her black traveling bonnet over her prayer *kapp,* and went out to hitch the buggy.

The midwife was Dora Smith, the same Amish midwife who'd delivered her into the world. Dora lived half an hour away, down some narrow winding roads. Amos had warned her that the roads were bad and had gotten worse over the last couple years. He'd offered to drive her but Anita had insisted on going on her own.

She stepped up into the buggy and took hold of the reins. Once she jiggled the reins slightly, the horse moved forward. She'd forgotten how much she enjoyed driving a buggy.

The journey to Mrs. Smith's house took her past Simon's property. She looked over at the house to see if she could see him, but there was no sign of him. The further away she got from Amos' house, the more she relaxed. The sunlight dappling on her skin through the trees, and the air gently tickling her face, gave her a sense of peace.

She finally saw the narrow dirt track to Dora Smith's house, off to the left. The track was up a slight rise and wouldn't have been wide enough for two vehicles to pass each other; luckily none was coming toward her.

She pulled up at the house to see Dora in the doorway waiting to greet her. She got down from the buggy, and Dora walked toward her.

"Hello, Anita. I saw you on Sunday, but I didn't get a chance to talk to you."

"How have you been?"

Dora reached out and grabbed one of her hands. "I've been well. And you?"

Anita nodded.

"Let's take a closer look at you and see how this *boppli* of yours is doing."

Anita went inside glad that her midwife would be someone she'd known all her life.

After she examined her, Dora said, "All looks good." She helped Anita sit up.

"Are you certain?"

"*Jah*. I've been doing this for a long time."

"I didn't realize that I'd been so worried about..."

"That's normal for first-time *mudders*. After you've had a few, you'll know what's normal and what's not."

Anita knew that this baby was possibly the only one she'd ever have. She was grateful that God had given her the chance to have a child. She knew a couple of married women who were never able to have children, and she knew that her child was a blessing from God.

"*Denke,* Dora." Anita heard hoofbeats. "You have a visitor?"

"That'll be my next appointment."

"Sounds like you're busy."

"I'm getting busier all the time."

When Dora led her outside, Anita nodded to Molly, a woman she knew from the community. She was a younger woman just newly married, and didn't look like she was having a baby at all. Anita wondered if Molly had told anybody yet that she was having a baby.

Anita got back into the buggy, and breathed a heavy sigh of relief. She knew in her heart her baby would be all right, but had still suffered pangs of worry. It was nice to hear from the midwife that everything seemed fine. She made her way down the narrow driveway and turned onto the road back home.

Anita was lost in her daydreams enjoying the cool breeze blowing against her face when the horse suddenly pulled to one side and she nearly fell out of her seat. Then, the horse came to an abrupt halt. She wondered whether it was a broken wheel.

When she got out of the buggy, she leaned down to see that the wheel was wedged into a rut. She took hold of the cheek straps of the horse's harness to walk him forward, but the horse could not make the buggy budge. Anita could see that the horse was trying. She let go of him and patted him on his neck.

"It's okay, boy. We'll just have to wait here until someone comes along. Hopefully someone will come along in a car and might be able to pull us out."

Anita leaned against the buggy so she'd be ready to wave a car or another buggy down. A few moments later, she saw a car.

She stepped out on the road a little way to wave it down.

The car pulled up beside her, and a man stuck his head out the window. "What's happened?"

She pointed to the back wheel. "The wheel's stuck. I can't budge it."

"I'll see what I can do." He pulled the car off to the side and got out to help her. He leaned down to study the wheel, and said, "Looks like it's stuck there good and proper. You get the horse to pull, and I'll push the back of the buggy."

After a few unsuccessful attempts, they both came to the conclusion that what they were doing was not going to work.

He rubbed his neck. "I don't know what else to do. Can I call someone for you? I've got a phone in the car."

"Yes please." She couldn't remember the phone number in Amos's barn, and the only thing she could think of was the name of Simon's business. "Are you able to look up a number for me?"

"Should be able to. What is it?"

"Watson Buggies, in town. Can you ask for Simon and tell him where I am?"

"Will do." The man headed to his car.

Anita listened in on the man's conversation and by the sounds of it he'd eventually gotten to speak to Simon. The man ended the call, and then got out of the car and called out, "He said he'd be here in fifteen minutes."

"Thank you for calling him. I appreciate it."

"Would you like me to wait with you?"

"That's nice of you, but I'll be all right here by myself."

The man gave a wave and got back into his car. Anita watched the car drive away. She was impressed how nice the man had been. She hadn't had a lot to do with *Englis-*

chers, but the ones she'd met had been kind to her.

It was a blessing that the man had come by, because no one had passed her until she saw Simon's buggy heading toward her.

"What trouble have you got yourself into?" he asked, a big grin on his face.

"It seems as though I'm stuck in a rut."

Simon jumped down from his buggy and examined the back wheel. Without a word, he went back to his buggy and brought back a shovel. "This should fix it." After minutes of shoveling, he placed the shovel on the side of the road. "Try to lead him forward."

Anita took hold of the horse's cheek strap, and clicked him onward. It was the same as before; the horse and the buggy went nowhere.

"It doesn't look like this is going to move. I'll get behind and push it." Once Simon was behind, he yelled, "Okay go."

The horse pulled, Simon pushed, and then they heard a loud 'crack.'

"That doesn't sound good," Anita said.

The buggy wheel had moved out of the rut, but now there was something wrong with it.

Simon called out, "Looks like there's damage to the wheel." He walked around the front to face her. "You'll have to drive it back nice and slow. Follow me back. I won't leave you, in case something happens again."

"Denke so much, Simon, for coming out. I hope you didn't mind me calling you, but I didn't know who else to call. I couldn't remember the number of Amos and Hannah's phone in the barn."

"I'm glad you called me. I haven't seen much of you lately." He leaned against the buggy. "Amos let me know I'm not too welcome over there at the moment."

Anita looked down and didn't want to ask why. When she looked up at him, she said, "He gets some crazy ideas in his head sometimes."

Simon folded his arms, and said, "What were you doing along these roads? These roads are never *gut,* especially after rain."

"I was heading back after seeing Dora Smith, the midwife."

"Is the *boppli* alright?"

Anita nodded. "She said everything's going fine. The *boppli* and I are well."

"That's good. I'm glad to hear it." He looked up at the gray sky. "We'd better start heading back before it rains again. I'm certain Amos won't mind me being on his property if it's to bring you safely back home."

"He'll be fine. He's like a big scary dog; his bark is worse than his bite."

Anita followed Simon's buggy back to Amos' house. She knew that Hannah would be at work and hoped that Amos would be out working on the farm somewhere so he wouldn't see Simon.

When Amos' house came into view, Anita was pleased that there seemed to be no one around the house. Simon brought his buggy right up to the barn where the buggies normally parked. After Anita stopped the buggy and climbed down, Simon came closer to have another look at the wheel.

"I'll have to have a closer look at it in better light."

Anita looked up at the overcast sky. It was darker than usual for that time of day.

Then Anita saw Amos making his way over to them from behind the house. "Into the *haus,* Anita," he yelled.

Anita looked in fright from Amos to Simon. She didn't want to be the cause of an argument and Amos seemed to be seething. "Why?"

"Because I'm going to have some private words with Simon."

Anita called out, "There's something

wrong with the buggy and Simon helped me with it. You might want to take a look at it."

"It's okay, Anita," Simon said in a quiet voice.

Anita looked over at Simon and he nodded toward the *haus*. Anita took a deep breath and walked away. Why was her brother such an unreasonable man?

When she walked into the house, she heard Amos' raise his voice at Simon. She went back outside and yelled, "Stop it, Amos! Stop it! Your buggy is broken, and Simon was helping me get it out of a rut. He helped me bring it home."

When she stopped, she saw both men looking at her as though they'd never seen or heard a woman yell before. Tears trickled down her cheeks, and she said, "Can't you just stop it, Amos?"

Amos faced her with his hands on his hips. "How did he just happen to stop by to help you with the buggy?"

"It's okay. I'm going," Simon said backing away. "She's getting upset, Amos."

"I can see that. She's my *schweschder!*" Amos yelled at him.

Simon got in his buggy and turned it around. Anita went back inside the house. She walked into the living room sat down and tried to make herself stop crying.

Amos came in and sat down in front of her.

Through her tears, Anita said, "Somehow the buggy got trapped in a rut. A man stopped to help me and couldn't get it out. He asked me if I wanted to call someone. I couldn't remember your number; the only thing I remembered was the name of Simon's business. The man looked it up and called Simon to help me. That's the only reason Simon came out. Was I supposed to just wait there until you realized I was late and came looking for me? We're not lying. Do you think we were meeting in secret or something?" Anita took a deep breath. "Can't you see for yourself that there's something wrong with the buggy?" Anita wiped the tears away from her face with the back of her hand.

They were interrupted by sounds of a buggy.

"Sounds like Hannah coming home."

When Hannah walked into the room without the children, she told Amos that her mother was looking after them overnight.

Amos' lips drew together tightly and Anita knew he wasn't happy about the children staying overnight. Anita wondered how long he would let Hannah keep her job.

When Hannah looked at Anita she rushed to her side, "What's wrong? Is the *boppli* all right?"

"The *boppli* is fine."

Hannah glared at her husband. "Have you done something to upset her?

Amos lifted his chin high. "I'll tell you

about it later, but right now it's time to cook the evening meal, isn't it? You know I don't like to eat my food too late in the night."

Hannah nodded, and said to Anita, "Come and talk to me while I cook."

Anita pushed herself up from the chair and went into the kitchen with Hannah.

"Now tell me what's the matter," Hannah ordered.

Anita told her all that had happened.

Hannah shook her head. "Amos has got a *gut* heart."

"I know he has. I'm trying to do what he wants because he thinks he's looking after me. But your *bruder* did not have any bad intentions, and neither did I. He assumed that Simon and I did something wrong."

Hannah nodded. "I know."

Anita dabbed at her eyes with her fingertips. "Normally I never cry."

"You're going through an emotional time. I cried all the time when I was carrying Sam."

Hannah laughed. "That is, when I wasn't being sick."

"At least I'm over the morning sickness. That was dreadful. Tell me, how did you enjoy your first day?"

A smile glimmered on Hannah's face. "It was *wunderbaar.* It was so busy. There were two buses that stopped outside and the place flooded with people."

"It must be nice to do something a little different from being home all the time."

"It was. I think two days will be all I can do, though, with everything I've got to do around here."

"If you want to do more, I can help around here and with the boys. As long as it's all right with Amos," Anita said.

Hannah giggled. "*Nee,* I think I'm happy with two days, and I wouldn't like to push things with Amos." Hannah handed Anita a basket. "Let's go outside and get some vegetables for dinner. I've got salted pork, and we can cook up some vegetables with it."

Since the boys were with their grandmother, Anita thought it would be a good time to have a talk with Amos over the way he was treating Simon.

After they said their silent prayers, Anita said, "I don't know why you've stopped Simon from coming here. He's only been a good friend to me."

"You can't call him a friend. You hardly know the man. He would've been just a *bu* when you left here; and you've only been back a short while."

"That's not fair to say. He's Hannah's *bruder,* and I've seen him quite often. His intentions towards me are nothing other than being a friend. We're part of the same *familye.* I don't know why you can't see that."

"I've told you before why I think that."

Hannah interrupted, "What do you mean, Amos? Are you keeping something from me?" Hannah looked at Amos, and then glanced at Anita.

Amos set his knife and fork down, pressed his hands together, and set his elbows on the table. When he finally spoke, he said, "I told Anita I've seen the way he looks at her, and it's not how someone would look at their *schweschder.*"

"What does that matter, then? You think Anita should be married, so what's wrong with my *bruder?"*

"He's younger! There are much better matches for her."

Hannah scowled. "Who? Mark Yoder, or his older *bruder,* Hans?"

Amos drew his dark eyebrows together. "Not Hans. I already told Anita he's too old, but Mark would be her best match."

Anita didn't know where to look. She glanced at Hannah, to see her staring at her husband looking none too happy. Anita held her head in her hands. She had only meant to have her brother be nice to Simon, not set husband and wife against each other. "I didn't mean to cause an argument," Anita said as she looked at Amos. "Can't you see, Amos, I'm not interested in any man?"

Amos shook his head.

Anita continued her explanation, "Maybe in a few years I might feel differently, but not now. I don't have to live here, I can move out somewhere by myself. I don't like to cause irritations."

"You're welcome to live here forever. This is your home; I want you to feel as though it's your home," Amos said.

Anita saw her brother's eyes become watery.

"Thank you, Amos. Forget I mentioned anything. Let's just put this behind us. All I want is for my *boppli* to be brought into this world happy and healthy. Simon has done nothing wrong, and he's Hannah's *bruder.* Can't you see if me being here is causing upsets, I'll have to stay somewhere else? Amos, please tell me you realize that."

He nodded.

"Does that mean Simon's welcome back here?" Anita closed her eyes and hoped she hadn't pushed him too far. She opened her right eye to see Amos raise his hands in the air.

"Let's just leave things how they are at the moment. And I don't want to hear another word about Simon at this dinner table tonight."

"Libby is having a candy stall at the Mud Sale," Hannah said.

"When's that on? I love mud sales," Anita said.

"Three weeks time. I happen to know who'll be running the auction." Hannah smiled at Anita.

When Amos cleared his throat loudly, Anita knew that it was Simon who'd be running the auction.

CHAPTER 11

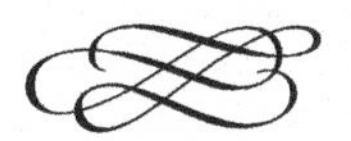

Thy faithfulness is unto all generations: thou hast established the earth, and it abideth.
Psalm 119:90

It was weeks later, and they were at the Mud Sale, and it wasn't called a mud sale for no reason. Anita looked down to see clumps of mud stuck on her black boots. She had to be careful where she stepped so she wouldn't slip.

Hannah had gone ahead earlier with Libby, and Anita had arrived with Amos and the boys. Amos took the boys to look at something while Anita looked for Hannah and the candy stall.

"There you are. I've been waiting for you to come. Where are the boys?"

"They're with Amos somewhere. I'm sure they'll be by later." Anita ran her gaze over the candies. She selected three bags of hard caramels, her favorite. "Are you here all day?" Anita asked when she handed Hannah the money.

"I'm here most of the day, but I do get a break for lunch at twelve."

"I'll tell Amos when I see him. He'd like to have lunch with you."

When more people came to the stall, Anita walked away to give them some room to view the candy.

Anita heard the auction start in the main arena. She walked over, and when Simon came into view she leaned her back against a post to watch him. Anita figured she was far enough away so Simon wouldn't be able to see her. After half an hour of standing, she spotted a seat open up in the back row, so she sat down. Simon handled the job of auctioneer very well, and Anita knew it couldn't be his first time at it. He certainly was a handsome man; Anita could see why many girls in the community were fond of him.

When the auction was over, Anita walked away with the crowd leaving their seats. She had just bought an ice cream and was leaning against a tree eating it when she spotted Simon. He saw her at just the same moment, and made his way over to her.

"Have you been here all day?" he asked.

"I've been here for a good while. I watched you for a little while at the auction. You did well."

He grinned and looked down. "Think so?"

Once his eyes were fixed on hers again, she nodded.

"Are we allowed to be speaking with each other?" he said as he looked around.

"We'll soon find out. Here he comes," Anita said.

"There you are." Amos said looking at both of them. "Let's go and have lunch."

Simon's eyebrows shot up. "Me too?"

Amos slapped him on the back. "Of course. Why not?"

Simon looked at Anita, and then smiled. "I'd love to have something to eat."

They both followed Amos to the food tent.

Hannah was having a break from the candy stall and had saved them a table. Ben and Sam were sitting at the table with her. They all sat, ate, and had polite conversation.

"Do you think you'd be able to take a look at that buggy wheel for me, Simon?" Amos asked.

"*Jah* I could. I'd be happy to."

"Come over tomorrow and have a look at it."

"What have you been using? You haven't been using that buggy I hope."

"We've got a second one, but it's old."

"I never knew you had a second one," Simon said.

"He's kept it at the back of the barn covered in burlap sacks. There's nothing wrong with it, it was Amos and Anita's *vadder's* buggy," Hannah said. "And you must come over to dinner tomorrow night just like old times."

Simon glanced at Amos. "I'd like that, as long as it's okay with you, Amos."

When everyone looked at Amos, he then said, "That would be all right."

When lunch was over, Hannah went back to her candy stall and Amos and the boys were ready to go home. "I've got to take the boys home for a sleep, Anita. Do you want to come home with me now? You could wait here and I'll collect you when I come back to get Hannah at closing time."

"I think I'd like to stay on," Anita said.

Simon said, "If she gets tired I could bring her home."

Amos looked at Simon and gave him a nod.

When Amos walked away with the two boys, Anita giggled. "That was very brave of you," she said to Simon.

"*Jah,* I know. I wasn't expecting him to agree. Have you said something to him to bring about his change of mind about me?"

"*Nee,* I haven't."

"You best stick with me, then. In case you get tired and I have to take you home." He smiled at Anita and she smiled back at him.

Anita liked his company and she knew he felt the same way.

"Shall we walk to the far end and see what's over there?"

"Let's go," Anita said.

They were making their way past one of the many tents where people were having tea and coffee when they saw the bishop's wife, Fran, sitting by herself. "Do you think I should go over and ask why I wasn't on that list?" Simon asked.

Anita's fingertips flew to her mouth as she laughed. "Don't you dare!"

He stopped walking and she stopped too. "And how are you doing with that list? Have you chosen anyone yet?" he asked.

"I completely forgot about the list, and I don't even know where it is."

"That's very careless of you. Fran was good enough to go to the trouble to make a list for you; the least you could've done was given it some serious consideration."

Anita saw Simon's eyes sparkle with mischief. "Come on." Simon held the back of her arm, and started walking toward Fran.

"Stop it," Anita said with a laugh, but it

was too late, Fran had looked up to see them walking over.

As they approached, Fran motioned to the spare chairs at her table. "Sit with me. I'm all alone."

"Denke. We will," Simon said, pulling out a chair for Anita.

When they sat down, Fran was quick to say, "Tell me how you two are getting along?"

Before Anita or Simon could say anything, Fran added, "I wouldn't have placed you two together."

"He's my *bruder*-in-law. He's Hannah's *bruder*." Anita looked over at Simon to see a huge smile on his face; it was clear that he was enjoying every moment of her embarrassment.

Fran shook her head and patted Anita's hand. "He's only a *bruder*-in-law by marriage. He's once removed, or is it twice removed? I can never get these things straight. He's no relative of yours, not directly, it's only because his *schweschder* married your *bruder*." Fran tapped on her chin. "I remember that Hosea Burkholder married Elsa King, and then her *bruder* married Hans' *schweschder.* That kind of thing happens all the time. It's not a problem. Do the two of you want to make a time to see John? You've plenty of time before the next wedding season and the *boppli* will be here by then, but it doesn't hurt to have the wedding arrangements made a long time before. It's always best to be prepared than wait until the last moment."

Simon leaned forward. "*Nee* we're not ready to talk to John yet, but you are right about us not being related in any way except by my *schweschder's* marriage to Anita's *bruder.*

Fran looked back at Anita. "See, my dear? There's nothing to stand in your way. And he such a lovely young man." Fran smiled adoringly at Simon.

"Thank you, Fran," Simon said.

Anita had to put her straight. What would happen if Fran mentioned something to Amos? "You've got this all wrong, Fran. There's nothing between us, we're only friends."

Fran smiled, and nodded. "I won't say a thing. You can rely on me. Now are you two going to keep me company by having a cup of tea?"

Simon stood up. "I'll get it. Will you have another cup, Fran?"

She shook her head. "*Nee,* I've not finished this one yet."

Simon looked over at Anita. "Tea for you?"

"*Kaffe* please."

Fran leaned over to her. "I don't know if you should be drinking *kaffe.*"

"I think a little bit's all right, and I haven't had any today yet. *Kaffe* please, Simon."

When Simon went to get the drinks, Fran whispered to Anita, "You're quite blessed you know. I don't know how many girls we've had crying over at the *haus* because he won't pay them any mind."

"Crying, over Simon?"

Fran nodded.

"He's popular?" Anita stared after him. She could see why he'd make the young girls cry. He was handsome, hard-working, and he had a lovely and pleasing personality. "I guess I can understand why." *He's everything that I would want in a man, if I were young again and single.*

She was tempted to tell Fran again that she wasn't interested in the man, but she knew there was no use.

"I know you're thinking it's too soon to tell anyone, but no one will mind. Judge not lest ye be judged, I'd say to them. There's nothing wrong with marrying again after you lose one man. *Gott* made us to want company, and for every man to have a woman and every woman to have a man."

She leaned further over, and whispered, "It's better to keep sin from the door rather than trying to shut the gate after the horse has gotten away."

The shock of what Fran said made Anita giggle. She hoped Fran wouldn't think she was being rude, but she couldn't help but laugh. Simon came back with the hot drinks, and saved Anita from having to explain to Fran why she'd just laughed in her face.

"Denke, Simon."

"What are you two laughing at?" Simon asked.

"Fran was just giving me something to think about." Anita took a sip of coffee. "And I didn't mean to laugh, Fran."

Fran patted Anita's hand, before she turned her attention to Simon. "How's your business going, Simon? Thriving, is it?"

"Jah, it's going really well. I can't complain."

"I'd think you wouldn't want to complain.

Seems everything's going well for you." She looked at Anita. "And for you too."

Anita smiled.

"And you just bought that lovely big *haus.* It's way too big for just you, Simon, with all those extra rooms."

"*Jah*. As soon as I marry, we'll fill it up with *kinner* as fast as we can."

Simon teasing Fran backfired, when Fran pointed to Anita's tummy, and said, "And you've got a head start on the *kinner* already."

Anita smiled and had to shake her head.

Fran pulled her attention away from them when she spotted someone she knew. "There's Vera over there." She looked at each of them in turn. "Mind if I leave you two here?"

"We don't mind at all," Simon said.

Anita knew that Vera and Fran were the best of friends. When Fran left the table, Anita leaned over, and said to Simon, "I hope she's not going to tell Vera about our secret relationship."

Simon looked over at Fran scurrying toward Vera. "Of course she is. What else would they have to talk about?"

Anita laughed. "She told me you've upset quite a few girls in the community, and made them cry. "

Simon put his hand on his chest. "I have?"

"That's what Fran said."

He frowned. "How have I upset anyone?"

"It appears you've been ignoring them, or some such thing."

Simon's cheeks reddened, and he took a mouthful of coffee. When he set the cup back on the saucer, he said, "There's not much I can do about that."

Anita wondered why some girl hadn't taken his eye. "You've not come across anyone in the community you like?"

"The truth is, I haven't." He looked into her eyes. "Not until now."

Anita gulped hard. She hadn't expected him to say that. She thought he might be fond of her, just as she enjoyed his company. Anita was both concerned and flattered at the same time. She put her fingers to her throat searching for something to say.

"I didn't mean to embarrass you. I thought I should be honest about my attraction to you just in case you might feel the same one day, when you're ready."

How could she explain that she did like him, but it was too soon, and besides that she still loved Joshua?

He chuckled. "Forget I said anything. Let's just enjoy one another's company."

Tears came to Anita's eyes and she did her best to blink them back.

He handed her a paper napkin.

"*Denke.* I don't know why I'm crying. I don't normally cry."

"I wasn't even ignoring you. Apparently that's usually how I make girls cry."

Anita gave a laugh as she dabbed at the corners of her eyes with the napkin. "I'd like us to be friends, and I think that we can, now that Amos is letting you come back to the *haus.*"

"Now that I've opened my big mouth about how I feel, I might as well go the whole way. I know your husband has just been taken from you suddenly, and I've no idea how that feels, especially in your condition. I'm going to put myself forward to you and say that if you ever find you might be interested in marrying again, I'd like you to consider me."

Anita laughed, but then saw that he was serious. "You're so young, Simon."

"Age is nothing but a number. Once someone reaches maturity, he's an adult. I guess there's something to be said for experience one gains with age, but experiences are nothing if one doesn't learn from them. I've learned from all mine."

Anita frowned. She couldn't quite follow what he was talking about, but he made more sense than Fran had, when she'd been talking about horses and shutting gates. Anita breathed out heavily. "I'll keep that in mind."

"I know you don't want to think about things like that right now, but I don't want to miss out if, and when, you ever consider another marriage. Neither do I want to put any pressure on you. I hope by saying all these things I haven't ruined our friendship. If we can only ever be friends, I'm more than happy with that."

"We haven't known each other long, but I do feel I've known you forever."

"Don't say anything further. I just wanted you to know how I feel. When Amos wouldn't let us speak, I had an awful feeling I might find out one day that you were about to marry one of the Yoders, or someone else who Amos thought would be suitable for you."

Anita nodded, pleased he wasn't putting any pressure on her. She liked him too, but if she told him too much he might expect something of her, and she had nothing to give. She was emotionally drained from everything she'd been through. Besides, she couldn't just switch off from one man and switch onto the next. Her heart needed to heal. "I'm glad you told me how you feel."

"That's all you need to say. I'm not asking for an answer." He looked over to a crowd of people to the left of them. He nodded his head toward Fran and Vera. "They're looking over at us."

"Ach nee. It'll be all over the community in no time."

Simon laughed.

Anita drank the last of her coffee.

"Finished?" Simon asked.

"Jah."

"Come on, let's see what else there is to see."

Simon and Anita spent the rest of the day together and when the Mud Sale came to a close, Simon walked Anita back to Hannah's candy stall. When they got there, Hannah was nowhere to be seen.

"Where's, Hannah?" Anita asked Libby.

"You've just missed her. She's just gone home."

"Did she go home with Amos?"

Libby nodded.

"Looks like I'll have the pleasure of your company while I drive you back home," Simon said.

"Denke, Simon. I wonder why they didn't wait for me. I said I was going home with them."

"They most likely thought you'd already left."

"I suppose so."

When Simon took her home, he didn't go

inside the *haus.*

Anita pushed the door open.

"Anita, there you are," Hannah said.

"I just missed you. I got there at closing time and Libby said you'd just left."

"I'm sorry, we thought you'd gone home already when we couldn't find you."

"Where's Amos?"

"He's putting the boys to bed."

Anita took off her shawl. "I thought that was your job."

"He said he'd do it because I've been on my feet all day."

Anita threw her shawl on her bed, and came back out to the kitchen. She grabbed one of the pieces of carrot that Hannah was cutting and popped it into her mouth. When she swallowed it, she picked up another piece, and said, "That was nice of Amos to put the boys to bed."

"He's been very thoughtful lately."

"Gut."

"I saw you spending a lot of time with Simon today."

Anita sat down at the table. "*Jah,* he's good company."

"He does like to look at the funny side of things. He's always been a joker."

"What can I do to help, Hannah?"

"You could shell the peas."

Anita walked over to the sink and brought the peas back to the table. She sat back down and began to shell them. "I'm glad that Amos and Simon have mended their differences."

"I guess you would be." Amos stuck his head around the kitchen door.

"Aren't you supposed to be putting the boys to bed?" Anita asked.

"They're already asleep. I couldn't get them to sleep this afternoon. I think the Mud Sale had them too excited."

Amos took a seat at the table. "I know I've

been stubborn about Simon, but now I see that you two are just friends."

"That's good," Anita said, not knowing why he'd come to think that and not game to ask. "We're just friends," she confirmed.

"I do think you should keep your mind open to the possibility of finding another *mann.*"

"Amos! I think Anita's had enough talk on that subject. You know she's not happy about you trying to match her with Mark Yoder."

He looked up at his wife. "I didn't have Mark Yoder in mind. I've just heard that Eli Smith is coming back to the community."

CHAPTER 12

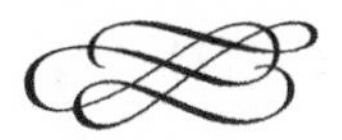

Thou wilt shew me the path of life: in thy presence is fulness of joy; at thy right hand there are pleasures for evermore.

Psalm 16:11

"Really?" Hannah pulled out a chair and sat down at the table. "Wasn't he a *gut* friend of yours years ago, Anita?"

Anita was still a bit shocked; Amos had

just announced that Eli Smith was coming back to the community.

Anita frowned at Hannah, wondering how she could possibly remember that she'd been friends with Eli. "*Jah,* he was a close friend before I married and moved away. Then I heard he married someone not long after and moved from here."

"His *fraa* died nearly a year ago. He's coming back."

"To live, or for a visit?" Anita asked.

"He's coming for a visit and he said he might stay on."

"That would be lovely. Where's he staying?" Anita popped a couple of fresh peas into her mouth.

Amos looked away from her and rubbed the back of his neck. "He's staying here."

Anita clenched her jaw. "How long have you known this?"

He looked across at her and blinked a couple times. "I got a letter from him today saying he's leaving to come here in a few days."

"I didn't know you two were such *gut* friends."

"Well, we are." Amos gave a sharp nod.

"So he's been visiting here since he left?"

"He's been back for weddings and funerals and the like."

Anita remained silent feeling a little guilty for not making the journey to come to Amos and Hannah's wedding. "I'll be happy to see him again."

"That'll be nice, won't it, Anita? The two of you have both lost loves and you'll have that in common too."

Anita nodded. *"Jah,* it'll be nice to have someone to talk to about things that you have to experience to understand." Anita continued to shell the peas. "Does he have any *kinner?"*

Amos said, "She died in childbirth, his *fraa* did."

Anita gasped.

"Amos, you didn't have to tell her that," Hannah said.

"It's the truth, woman." Amos scowled at Hannah.

Hannah shook her head at him, then rubbed Anita's arm. "Don't worry; that hardly ever happens."

"How sad for him. And the *boppli* died too?" Anita asked.

Amos nodded, glanced at Hannah, and then said, "Seems I'm not allowed to tell you the details."

Anita shook her head, and then covered her ears with the palms of her hands. "*Nee.* Don't tell me." Anita didn't want to have such things in her head before she faced the unknown event of her first childbirth.

"Amos, go and read in the living room. Leave Anita and me in peace while we get the meal ready."

Amos chuckled. "All right. I'll leave you

two alone so you can have your women's talk." He pushed out the chair causing it to screech along the floorboards. Then he stood up, placed the chair back under the table, and strode out of the room.

"Sorry, Anita."

"That's okay. He didn't know it would upset me, I suppose. I'm nervous. I don't know about childbirth. I've heard about it, but that's all. Some say it doesn't hurt and then other women say it does."

"The best thing is not to think of it as pain. It's good pain. It's your body opening up for your baby to enter the world."

Anita nodded. "That helps, I think."

"Do you want me to come with you? I could be the birth-helper."

"Would you?"

"I'd love to, if you want me to."

"I'd like nothing more." Tears came to Anita's eyes again. "Oh *nee.* I'm crying again. This isn't like me. I haven't cried for years. I cried when Joshua died, I mean I cried for days, but before that, I hadn't cried for years."

"Here." Hannah handed her some paper napkins. "It's only normal to feel sad, then happy, then sad all in the space of five minutes when you're expecting."

Anita sniffed.

Hannah gathered up the peas Anita had shelled and put them into the pan with the other vegetables.

"When is Eli coming?"

"He'll be here in a few weeks. That's what Amos told me earlier."

Hannah seemed to know more than she was letting on, which led Anita to wonder again if husband and wife were both setting her up. Were they trying to match her with Eli? And if so, did Eli know of it? "So you knew the two of them were good friends, Eli and Amos?"

"I don't know. He just told me about Eli

coming to visit and said that he might stay on. I remembered that the two of you were good friends before you married Joshua."

"That was a long time ago."

"*Jah,* that was before Amos and I married."

CHAPTER 13

And said, Verily I say unto you, Except ye be converted,
and become as little children,
ye shall not enter into the kingdom of heaven.
Matthew 18:3

Three weeks later, Anita was outside playing with the boys when she heard Hannah call out, "He's here."

"Come on, you two. Come and meet *onkel*

Eli," Anita said to the children. She took their hands and they walked around the front of the house.

Anita and the boys joined Hannah and Amos waiting out in front of the house. A taxi pulled up and Eli got out. Amos helped him get his luggage out of the trunk. He had four large suitcases.

Must be everything he owns, Anita thought.

He looked exactly the same as he had all those years ago. He greeted everyone and then bent down and shook hands with Ben and Sam. Then Amos ushered everyone into the house.

"I'll carry your things up to your room. Let's sit for a while first, and you can tell us what you've been doing," Amos said.

When Eli took off his hat, Anita saw that his hair was graying around his temples.

"Everyone sit down. I'll get us something to eat." Hannah had everyone sit in the living room.

"I'll help," Anita said heading to the kitchen behind Hannah.

"*Nee,* get away with you. You go and sit down. It's all ready. I just have to carry it out."

When Anita sat in front of Eli, she noted that his face was clean-shaven, meaning he was probably looking for a wife, as all married men and new widowers had beards.

"I hear your husband's recently gone to be with *Gott?*"

Anita nodded. "And I heard about your *fraa.* I was sad to hear about what happened."

"It's all *Gott's* will."

Anita nodded, noting his stoicism and saying nothing of the pain of losing her husband.

"Here we go," Hannah said as she placed the tray of coffee and cakes down on the table between the two couches.

"This looks *gut,*" Eli said.

"What kind of work have you been doing, Eli?" Hannah asked as she sat down.

"I make furniture."

"That's right," Anita said. "I remember you were always good with working with wood."

Eli chuckled. "I learned from my *grossdaddi.*"

"There'd be plenty of call for that around these parts if you stay on," Amos said.

"I've never been short of work."

Hannah passed Eli a slice of cake.

"Denke, Hannah."

Eli looked over at the boys playing in the corner of the room. "You've got two fine boys over there." He looked over at Anita. "And you've been blessed too."

"Jah, I've not got long to go."

"Only weeks away, isn't it?" Amos said.

Anita nodded.

"We'll have to get the *grossdaddi haus* ready. We haven't even got a crib for you."

"Anita can use, Sam's, he's grown out of it."

"Denke, I will take *gut* care of it."

"Would you allow me to make you a crib, Anita?"

"Nee, I couldn't allow you to do that."

"The man wouldn't have offered if he didn't want to do it, Anita." Amos said sternly as though she was being rude by not accepting his offer.

"It will give me something to do while I'm here besides helping Amos on the farm." He looked over at Amos. "I intend to earn my keep while I'm living here."

Living here? Anita breathed out heavily. *How long is he intending to stay*? When everyone stared at Anita, she said to Eli, "Are you certain you want to?"

"I would like very much to make one for you."

When he smiled at her she remembered the friendship they'd once shared. Although his hair was flecked with gray at the sides, he still had the same vivid blue eyes.

"Then I accept. *Denke.*" Anita hadn't wanted him to make her a crib because she didn't want people to force them together as they had tried to force Mark Yoder onto her. Making a crib for her might make Eli think they had a chance of a future together. While she thought on the things that Eli or others might think of her, she realized that the conversation had continued.

"What do you think about that, Anita?" Amos asked.

"I'm sorry. My mind was elsewhere."

"What would you think about Eli moving here, staying on in the community?"

"I think it would be *wunderbaar,* if that's what he decides he wants to do."

Eli smiled at her.

When they'd finished their conversation and all the cake and coffee were gone, Amos stood up. "I'll take your things up to your room, Eli. It's the first on the left up the stairs."

When Hannah bounded to her feet too, Anita knew beyond a doubt they were trying to match them together.

Hannah said, "I'll take these." She leaned over, picked up the tray and disappeared into the kitchen.

She stared at Eli wondering what to say to him. It would be awkward with him in the house, and worse still that she'd said 'yes' to him making her a crib.

"You haven't changed at all, Anita.

Anita gave a laugh to cover the awkwardness she felt inside. "I'm sure that's not so. I'm much older than when we last saw each other."

"The years have been kind to you."

"You certainly look the same," Anita said hoping it didn't sound like she was saying it only because he said it to her first. "What made you think of coming back to the community, Eli?"

"There aren't many women where I was."

Anita looked away. She'd been right all along. Anita pushed herself up out of the chair. "Well I think I should go and see how Hannah is getting along. I can't let her do everything herself."

"Before you go, Anita."

He grabbed her hand and Anita instinctively pulled away from him because it had given her such a fright that he'd touched her.

"Can you spare some time for me tomorrow?"

"Tomorrow?" Anita quickly tried to come up with an excuse so she wouldn't have to be alone with him.

"I'd like you to come with me to choose the wood for the crib."

Agreeing to that crib was a bad idea. "What wood is normally used?"

"There are several kinds. I'd really like

you to come with me and choose the wood. Let's do that together, shall we?"

"*Jah,* of course I'll come with you to choose the wood."

Eli smiled, and then Anita walked into the kitchen wondering what she'd gotten herself into. She nearly ran into Hannah who was very close to the door. "Were you listening in?" she whispered to Hannah.

Hannah put her hand over her mouth and giggled. Anita gave her a slap on the shoulder. "Stop it; it's not funny. He wants me to go and choose wood for the crib when I could just use your crib. I don't need a new one at all."

"He seems a very nice man and he obviously likes you."

"*Jah.* He's a nice man and I keep telling everybody I don't want any man, not at the moment. I just need time to get over the fact that Joshua isn't here any more. Don't you see that, Hannah? I can't ever forget about

Joshua. If something happened to Amos would you be able to just forget about him, and switch to another man?"

"*Jah,* probably. I think I could." Hannah laughed.

Anita shook her head. "You're impossible."

"Look, Anita, the man likes you, and wants to make your baby a crib. Where's the harm in that?"

"I don't want him to think that something more can happen between us. I don't like him that way, and have never liked him in that way. I never liked him as more than a friend."

"Why? I thought you'd like him. What do you find wrong with him?"

"Stop!"

Hannah walked passed her and continued washing the dishes.

"I'll help you in here, and then I might go for walk."

Hannah drew her hands out of the sudsy water and looked at her. "You never go for a walk."

"I need to get out by myself for a little bit."

"Okay. I'll go out and talk to our guest so he doesn't feel like he's been abandoned."

"Good thinking."

When Anita finished her duties in the kitchen, she threw her cape around her shoulders and left by the door in the *grossdaddi haus.* When she stepped outside, she hurried away just in case anyone saw her and tried to stop her.

She headed in the direction of Simon's house. Anita smiled as she remembered playing in the very same fields when she was a young girl. She'd had fun playing with her younger brothers and the other children in the community. And now, soon, her child could play in the very same fields with Sam and Ben, when he or she was old enough.

Anita stopped walking when she felt sharp pain in her chest. Dora, the midwife, had warned her she might get some heartburn, as the baby was growing larger. Dora had also told her to eat small meals and more often. Maybe she shouldn't have had such a large piece of cake.

She took a deep breath in, and kept walking. When she found a grassy spot, she sat down. Her eyes fell to the wildflowers in front of her and she recalled the daisy chains she used to make as a child. She plucked the yellow and white flowers until she had a handful, and then she carefully made a daisy chain. Anita placed the chain on her head just as she'd done when she was a child.

Out of the corner of her eye, she saw movement and hoped it wasn't one of the cows in the wrong paddock again. It was Simon on a horse. He waved to her and turned his horse toward her. When he was close, he jumped down and led the horse behind him.

"Hello," Anita said.

Simon bowed. "What are you doing so far away from your palace, your majesty?"

When she looked confused, he pointed to the top of her head. She remembered the daisy chain. She felt heat rise to her cheeks, and then she laughed as she ripped it off her head. "I forgot about this. I just felt the need to get away from the *haus.*" She glanced at the horse. "I've never seen you ride before."

"I'm riding the boundary fences to see what fencing work I've got coming up. There are always fences to be repaired."

Anita recalled her father often grumbling about repairing fences. "They look pretty good to me when I've driven past."

"That's because I've replaced most of them. When I bought this place, they were in a dreadful state. Mind if I sit?"

"Please do."

After he sat down, he asked, "Did I see a taxi heading to your place a few hours ago?"

"*Jah.* Our visitor arrived."

"Is that why you're out here walking?"

Anita giggled. "It might be."

"Is that Eli something or other? Eli Smith, isn't it?"

"*Jah* that's him. He's related to the midwife, Dora Smith, her grand nephew I think. Eli was a good friend of mine many years ago."

Simon raised his eyebrows in an exaggerated manner.

Anita giggled. "It's nothing like that."

"I've been meaning to ask you something."

"*Ach nee!* What is it? I don't like it when people start off their question like that. Okay what is it?"

"I need a woman's advice on paint."

"Paint? Paint for what?"

"I need to paint my living room and kitchen. You'd know what the best color would be." He smiled and looked into her eyes.

"Red is a good color." Anita knew no one in the community would ever use bright colors like that in their home.

"See! I knew you had good taste."

Anita laughed. "I'll be happy to help you choose a color."

"I'll come by tomorrow and collect you."

Anita remembered that she was supposed to go with Eli tomorrow to look at wood. "What about the day after?"

He nodded. "The day after it is. Hannah seems to like her job."

"Jah, she does."

"She told me you helped her with Amos over it."

"I'm sure he would've come around in the end, when he saw how much it meant to her."

"I don't know about that. He can be a little stubborn sometimes."

Anita looked up at the sky when she felt droplets of rain. She held her hand out. "Looks like I should head back."

"I'll walk with you." Simon stood up.

"Nee, it's okay. You continue looking at your fences, or whatever it was you were doing."

Simon chuckled and offered his hand. She took hold of it, and he pulled her to her feet. "Okay. I'll come by the day after tomorrow mid-morning. Don't you forget now."

"I won't." Anita walked away, pleased that she'd talked to him. He always made her feel better.

CHAPTER 14

Thou wilt keep him in perfect peace, whose mind is stayed on thee: because he trusteth in thee.
Isaiah 26:3

The following day was Thursday, and everyone was sitting around the table eating breakfast. Hannah was due to work in the candy store later that day.

"Are you sure you don't need the buggy today?" Hannah asked Anita.

Anita looked across the table at Eli. "Eli was going to take me to look at wood today."

Amos said, "Eli, why don't you take the buggy? You can take Hannah to work and drop the boys at her *mudder's*. That way you can both take the buggy for the day."

"Denke, Amos. That sounds like a mighty fine idea."

Anita wondered why Eli hadn't arranged something before now, but then again, she hadn't thought of how they'd look at the wood without borrowing the buggy either. Even though Amos had the spare buggy, and more than one horse, he never liked to use the older buggy.

"I'll get ready as soon as we clear up," Anita said.

"You ladies leave the cleaning up for me to do."

Both ladies stopped in their tracks and stared at Amos.

"Really?" Hannah asked.

"I don't have much work to do today. I do have to make an early start of it tomorrow. You might be able to give me a hand tomorrow, Eli."

"I'd be happy to."

Not wanting Hannah to be late for work, Anita hurried to her room. She placed her black over-bonnet over her prayer *kapp* and took hold of her black shawl. It was so hard to know what the weather was going to be like in the early months of the year. One minute it was warm, and the next minute it could turn quite chilly.

After Anita brushed her teeth, she glanced up at her reflection. She ran her fingertips over some faint dark patches that had appeared. *Oh nee. That's what the midwife said might happen.* It seemed that all the things the midwife warned her might happen had started happening. First there was the heartburn, and now the dark splotches on her skin. *Serves me right for looking in the mirror, I suppose. If I didn't look, I wouldn't know they were there. I hope they go away after I have the boppli. I've always had such clear skin.*

She hurried through the door that led back into the kitchen. Hannah was at the front door getting the boys' shoes on. Anita looked through the front door to see that Eli was already waiting in the buggy.

"All done." Hannah stood up.

Anita took Sam's hand and led him outside, while Hannah followed with Ben. Eli jumped down and lifted the boys into the buggy.

Once they were all set to go, Amos stepped out of the barn and gave a wave.

"Wave at *Dat,*" Anita said to the boys.

The boys and Anita were in the back seat while Hannah and Eli were in the front. Anita lifted the little one up from his seat so he could wave to his father. The boys both waved to him.

"You're going to see your *grossmammi,*" Anita said to the boys.

Hannah turned around. "They love going to *Mammi's haus.*"

"We're going to see, *Mammi,*" Ben said.

"That's right. You're growing up into such a big boy. You look after your *bruder* today, won't you?" Anita said.

"Jah."

After they left Hannah's mother's house, Eli drove Hannah to the candy store.

"I'll be finished at five, Eli," Hannah said when she stepped down from the buggy.

"We'll be waiting," Eli said. He turned around to look at Anita. "Come sit in the front with me."

"Jah, I was just getting my shawl." Anita took her shawl with her and climbed into the front seat.

He moved the horse forward. "I've missed this town."

"*Jah.* I think we always feel a certain fondness for the place we've grown up."

Eli glanced over at her. "Were you pleased to come home?"

"I had mixed feelings." The truth was she felt as though she'd gone backward and not forward in her life. She didn't feel as though Eli would understand her thoughts so she kept them to herself. "I mean I moved away married and came back home alone."

"Life has its ups and downs. Now, have you thought what kind of crib you'd like?"

"*Nee.* I haven't thought much about it. I don't know enough about wood to make any kind of decision."

"We can work it out together."

When he glanced at her and flashed a smile, she knew she was in trouble. She regretted accepting his offer of making the crib. He obviously had an attraction to her, and although he was a nice man, she didn't feel anything toward him other than remnants of their old friendship. Would he expect some affection or commitment from her when he made the crib? Somehow she knew that he was only doing it because he saw her as his future wife. Anita was certain that Amos had something to do with that.

Eli glanced at her. "What kind of wood do you like?"

"I'm not certain. Would it be painted?"

"You could have it painted if you want, but real wood-lovers like to see the color and the grain of the wood."

"That makes sense. Whatever you think is best."

He tipped his hat back on his head. "You've got to have some opinions, Anita."

Anita hoped she wasn't making him angry. She had become careful what she said around Amos lately, but she excused him because he was her brother. Anita certainly didn't want a husband, or even a potential husband, that she had to worry about offending or upsetting. Anita shook her head at that thought. Everyone was pushing her to find another man, and now she found she'd been entertaining the idea.

"Do you feel okay? Do you want me to stop the buggy a while?" Eli asked.

"Nee, I'm okay, *denke.* I was just thinking we could look at the timber when we're at the lumber yard, and then I can say which one I like."

"Nee. It's rough wood; you won't be able to tell anything from that. I'll take you to a furniture store where you can see all the different kinds of wood."

"That sounds *gut."*

He stopped the buggy at a furniture store. Anita was quick to get out of the buggy before he got to the other side to help her down. It was a large Amish furniture store, which hadn't been there when Anita had lived in the area. "This building wasn't even here a few years ago."

"*Jah*, it seems as though it's fairly new." He pushed the door open for her, and she walked through. As they walked down the aisles of furniture, Eli pointed out all the different varieties of wood.

When they rounded the end of one of the aisles, Anita saw someone who looked like Simon. She focused more intently and saw that it was Simon. "Let's look over this way," she said pointing in the other direction. She did not want to let Simon see her with Eli.

"Good idea. There are cribs over there and you can see the different styles."

Anita made herself concentrate on choosing a crib that looked nice to her, when she heard a familiar voice behind her.

"Hello, Anita."

She swung around to see Simon. "Simon, I didn't know you were here."

Simon stared at Eli and Eli stared back at him.

"Simon, this is..." Anita's mind went blank as she searched for her friend's name.

Eli put his hand out. "I'm Eli Smith."

"I'm Simon, Hannah's *bruder.*" They shook hands.

"Jah, Hannah's *bruder,"* Anita mumbled.

"Is this what you had planned today?" Simon asked staring intently at Anita.

She knew she had put off their outing to choose paint for his house, and hadn't told him she was going somewhere with Eli.

"Jah. Eli's been kind enough to offer to make me a crib. He's showing me designs and all the different types of wood."

Anita was just about to ask Simon what had brought him into the store, but before she could say anything further, Simon said, "I'll leave you both to it, then." He nodded to Eli before he walked away.

Anita stood open-mouthed and watched Simon walk away.

"So that's Hannah's younger *bruder?"*

Anita nodded. "Do you remember him?"

"Barely. He was so much younger. He's much younger than both of us. I'm sure he would've been just a *boppli* when you married Joshua."

"He's only six years younger."

"Is there anything between the two of you? Tell me now so I don't waste any more of my time."

Anita studied his face. Could he tell that she was genuinely fond of Simon? She had to cover up the feelings that she didn't want to admit to herself. *"Jah,* you're right. He's much younger than both of us."

"I'm sorry, Anita, I just can't do this."

"Do what?"

"I can't make you a crib when you've got your eyes on someone else. I put a lot of effort into my furniture. I can't make it for you now."

Anita looked down at the ground. "Whatever you think is best. I guess we should head home."

Eli said nothing and walked out of the store in front of her. He didn't even hold the door open for her. When she reached the buggy he was already sitting in the driver's seat with his hands on the reins.

It was a tense trip home, and it was even tenser when they arrived home. With Amos out working in the fields and Hannah at the candy store, it was just the two of them.

"Would you like a cup of tea or *kaffe?*"

He looked up from his seated position on the couch, and lowered the Amish newspaper he'd been reading. "I can't do this any more." Eli jumped up, and placed the newspaper on the couch behind him.

"Do what?"

"You've changed, Anita. You're not the same girl I used to know. You're setting yourself up for heartache if you think that man we saw today would ever be interested in you."

"I haven't got my eyes on anybody, Eli. I keep telling everybody that I'm not ready for anything at this time in my life."

"That's not the impression your *bruder* gave me."

"Amos?"

"Seems I've come all this way for nothing. When Amos told me you needed a husband, I thought I could come in and be a *vadder* to your child, and husband to you, but you haven't welcomed me. I'm too old to chase you, or try to win you from another man."

Anita shrugged her shoulders reaching for words. Nothing came to mind.

"I'm going to pack my things, and then call a taxi." He left her, and trudged up the stairs.

"Where you going?" she called after him.

"Back home."

Anita collapsed onto the couch, hoping

that Amos wouldn't blame her for Eli's sudden disappearance. But, in a way, she was glad to be relieved of the pressure. Now, with him gone and not making a crib for the baby, she wouldn't have to worry about feeling obligated toward him.

Fifteen minutes later, Eli threw his suitcases down at the front door and strode to the barn. Anita guessed he was calling for a taxi to take him to the bus stop. When he came out of the barn, he waited on the porch. Anita was too scared of his anger to join him.

When the taxi came, Eli opened the front door to retrieve his suitcases, and then closed the door heavily behind him. Anita watched through the window as he got into the taxi.

When the taxi was out of sight, Anita was flooded with a sense of peace and relief. Although she didn't like seeing anybody upset, a heavy load had been lifted from her.

She walked upstairs and looked at the crib in Sam's room. *There's nothing wrong with that. That'll do nicely.* On her way back downstairs, she wondered if she'd also upset Simon. She deliberately hadn't told him what she was doing when he wanted to take her to look at the paint. Would he see her not telling him that she had a prior appointment with Eli as being deceptive? Would he still come by to collect her tomorrow as they had arranged? Anita hoped that he would.

When afternoon came, with Eli gone, it was left to Anita to collect Hannah from work.

Hannah was surprised to see Anita driving the buggy. Before they fetched the boys from Hannah's mother's house, Anita told Hannah everything that had happened that day.

CHAPTER 15

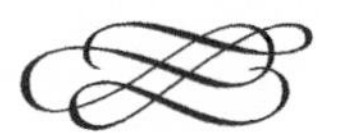

And the peace of God, which passeth all understanding, shall keep your hearts and minds through Christ Jesus.
Philippians 4:7

"What do you mean, Eli's gone?" Amos bellowed.

"Can't you see she's upset, Amos?" Hannah said.

Anita was helping Hannah mash vegetables for the boys' dinner. "He left and I don't know why. He didn't really say. He seemed to think I needed a husband and when I told him I wasn't interested, he became angry. He called a taxi and left." Anita shrugged her shoulders. She'd left out the part about running into Simon in the furniture store. The part she left out was her private business, and she didn't see why her younger brother should know every single thing about her life.

"Just like that? He just walked out, did he?

"Jah. That's right. You can ask him yourself. I didn't ask him to leave."

"I'll give him a couple of days to get home, and then I'll call him and find out for myself."

Hannah rounded her shoulders. "As you wish."

Amos stared at her as though he knew there was more to the story than what she was telling him.

Anita looked at Hannah. "Did you have a good day at work?"

Before Hannah could answer, Amos butted in, "You've surely talked about that on the way home in the buggy." Amos stood up from the kitchen table, and stomped out of the kitchen.

"He's upset," Hannah said.

Anita raised her eyebrows. "I can see that."

Ben and Sam were sitting at their small table. Hannah passed the boys a cooked carrot each to munch on while they were waiting on their mashed vegetables.

When Anita put the bowls of food in front of the boys, she said to Hannah,

"I need to go and speak to Amos about something." Anita walked out of the kitchen and sat in front of Amos.

He closed his paper up and looked at her.

"It's your fault you know."

Amos drew his eyebrows together. "What is?"

"It's your fault for telling a lie that I was interested in finding a husband. You know that's not true."

Amos looked away from her. "That's because you don't know what's good for you."

"What's good for me is to have a peaceful life, at least until my *boppli* comes into the world. I don't need to keep fighting you about this; I'm not interested in finding another husband. Joshua has only been gone a few months." Anita looked up to the ceiling and blinked rapidly to stop the tears from falling.

Amos stared at her and his mouth turned down at the corners. "I'm only trying to help you. If I don't help you, who else will?"

"I appreciate you wanting to help me, but can you wait to ask me if I want your help with something before you act next time?"

He gradually smiled. "I can do that."

"That'll make me feel much better."

He nodded, and then asked, "When do you go to see the midwife next?"

"I think I need to see her next Wednesday, and then after that, I see her weekly."

"She'll have to start coming here. You can't go driving over those bad roads by yourself."

There he was again being overprotective, but this time he was right, the roads were bad. She didn't want be stuck out on those roads again. "She did say at the later stages she'd come here"

"So she should. I'll take you there next week, and then we need to make sure that she comes here to see you."

"Denke, Amos."

Anita pushed herself to her feet, and went back into the kitchen to help Hannah with the dinner.

CHAPTER 16

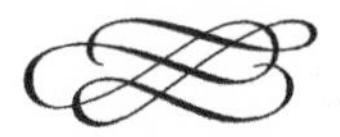

And walk in love, as Christ also hath loved us, and hath given himself for us an offering and a sacrifice to God for a sweetsmelling savour.
Ephesians 5:2

The next morning, Anita walked into the kitchen just after day-break. Hannah was already baking bread, and the two boys munched on something at their small table. "Amos has already left?" Anita asked.

"*Jah.* He wanted to get an early start."

"Eli was meant to help him today; that makes me feel bad."

"It was Eli's choice to leave. Do you have plans for the day?" Hannah asked Anita.

Anita sat down at the table wondering if Hannah knew her brother was coming by to take her somewhere. "Simon did mention that he might come by. He said he was going to take me somewhere, but I forget where."

Hannah laughed. "You're getting forgetful. I was like that during both my pregnancies."

"Were you?"

Hannah nodded, and Anita felt a little better. She was normally not forgetful; neither did she usually cry over small things.

It was mid-morning when Anita heard a horse and buggy making its way to the house. Her heart beat faster when she looked out the window to see that it was Simon. She was happy he hadn't been put off by her not being entirely truthful about the previous day.

"Sounds like he's here," Hannah called to Anita.

"I'm coming." Anita hurried to her room, placed her over-bonnet on, pulled her black shawl off the peg, and then came back into the main house. Anita kissed the boys, and said goodbye to Hannah. When she opened the front door, she came face-to-face with Simon.

"Hello, Anita. You're very rosy-cheeked today."

"Hello. I think it's the cold." She suddenly felt nervous and excited at the same time.

Simon looked into the house at Hannah, and gave her a wave. He called out to Hannah, "I'll come back later to play with the boys." He looked at Anita. "You ready?"

Anita nodded, and then they made their way out to his buggy.

Try as she might, Anita could not remember where he had said he was taking her. She hoped he'd mention where they were going soon.

As they traveled down the long driveway, Simon asked. "Eli helping Amos today?"

"Eli and I had a bit of a falling out, I'm afraid."

He whipped his head around to look at her. "What happened?"

"I upset him."

He was silent for a while before he said, "I find it hard to believe that you could upset anyone."

Anita grunted. "I think I've upset a few people since I've been here."

"Let me guess, one - Amos, and two – Fran?"

Anita giggled.

Simon took his eyes off the road for an instant to glance over at her. "Am I right?"

"I don't know if I've upset Fran too much, but you're right about Amos."

"Now tell me seriously, what did you do to upset Eli?"

"The whole situation was awkward. He insisted on making a crib for my *boppli* even though Hannah's got a perfectly good crib that she offered to loan me. I was put in a position where I couldn't say 'no.' Then he seemed a little annoyed that I didn't know what kind of wood I wanted or what style I wanted. I'm no expert on that kind of thing." Anita raised her hands in the air.

"And that's when he suggested taking you to the furniture store?"

"*Jah* that's right."

"And you didn't want him to make it because you didn't want to feel obligated to him?"

"That's exactly right." He seemed to understand how she felt, just like her friends back home in Ohio would. She missed her friends terribly. Back home she was always visiting her friends, or they were visiting her. They lived in out of each other's homes. She was happy to live with Amos and Hannah now, and not by herself. It was nice at night to know that there was someone else in the house. She had spent too many nights at home after Joshua had departed, alone with her grief and battling morning sickness, and they had been the worst nights she'd ever had.

Simon broke through her daydreams. "I hope you've given a lot of thought to the colors you're to choose today."

That's when Anita remembered. She was to help him choose paint for his house. "To be truthful, I haven't given any thought to it, at all."

"At least you're honest. Do you know how many shades of white there are?"

"Nee, I don't. How many are there?"

"There are about sixty different shades of white, so I'd hate to think how many different shades of cream there'd be. And then after we choose the color, we need to make the decision whether it's going to be flat, gloss, or semi-gloss. Then there's under-paint, over-paint, and the list goes on." Simon glanced over at her and smiled.

"Over-paint? Is that the same as normal paint?"

He shrugged, and then shook his head. "I'm no paint expert."

"I can see how difficult that would be; no wonder you need me to help you."

He wagged a finger at her. "And I'm trusting you to do a good job."

"I'll do my very best."

When they arrived at the paint store,

Anita was pleased that Simon rushed to help her down from the buggy.

They browsed through the paint cards, and then Anita decided on a color. "Do you think you should try a small portion of it on your wall first?"

"Is that what people do?" Simon asked.

"Only if it's an important decision for you. Or, if you're not sure about it."

Simon looked down at the sample paint card in his hand. "I think that'll do fine, and they tell me for walls it's best to choose a flat paint."

Anita nodded. Before long, the paint had been mixed, and Simon was loading two large cans into the back of the buggy.

He looked back at Anita. "You know you have to help me paint, don't you?"

Anita shook her head and put both hands on her tummy. "You'll be waiting a while if you want me to help you. Besides, I didn't say I'd help you paint."

"Fair enough. You'll have to come and watch me while I paint, then."

She shook her head. "Amos wouldn't approve."

Simon chuckled. "You're right about that, I guess."

"How about I come and look at it after you've painted it?"

Simon pulled a sad face. "I suppose that'll have to do. I'll tell you what, I'll let you get out of painting if you agree to have lunch with me right now."

"I could do with something to eat," Anita said.

SIMON TOOK them to a diner on the edge of town. They sat in the very back booth and looked through the menus. "Are you hungry?"

"I'm always hungry lately. Only thing is I

can't eat too much because I get heartburn. The midwife said I have to eat little bits, and often."

After the waitress took their order, Simon stared at Anita.

Anita laughed. "What is it that you're looking at?"

He laughed too. "Nothing."

"You can't laugh at me and then just say 'nothing.' Tell me what's so funny."

"I was just thinking about the situation your *bruder* got you into with Eli."

"I don't know if that's anything to laugh about." Anita grimaced. "He put me in a bad position. It was very embarrassing and probably more so for poor old Eli."

"Have you told your *bruder* how you feel?"

"I had a good talk with him last evening. He seemed to understand how I feel."

"Seemed to?" Simon cocked his head to one side.

"I'm confident he understands."

"Well, both you and Hannah must be wearing him down."

"He does have very definite opinions about things. So, when are you going to start painting?"

"I think I'll start tonight."

"Wouldn't it be better to wait for the warmer weather?"

"Nee. We always get busy at work in the summer months. And it doesn't matter too much if it takes a while to dry." He smiled and his eyes sparkled. "I'm in the big house all on my own."

Anita giggled when she remembered what Fran had said. "Fran seemed quite concerned that it's only you in that big house. Do you want me to have a word with her? She'd most likely love to write out a list for you as well."

Simon raised his hands. "Please don't."

Anita stared at him and wondered if he knew that many girls liked him. Fran had said that quite a few girls had come to her house in tears because he never gave them any attention.

"What are you thinking about? You've got that far-away look in your eyes."

"I was just thinking that it must be hard to be a bishop and have to listen to everybody's problems."

"Did you tell him your problems?"

Anita's eyes grew wide as she tried to recall exactly what she'd talked to the bishop about. "When I went to visit the bishop, we only talked for five minutes before he was called away. The rest of the time I spoke to Fran. That's when she gave me the list."

"That's right, and you tasted her chocolate cake. Did you ever get that recipe from her?"

"*Nee.* I haven't asked her about it again, but I have tried various cake recipes to try to make one that tastes the same."

"Any success?"

"Nowhere near it."

"Your big mistake was not getting the recipe right away when she said she'd give it to you."

Anita shrugged her shoulders. "I can't turn back the clock."

The waitress placed their plates in front of them.

Anita stared down at the burger and fries on the over-sized plate. "I don't think I'll be able to get through all of this."

Simon picked up his burger with both hands. "Aren't you eating for two?"

"I've been extremely hungry, but this is far too much. You might have to help me out with this lot."

Simon had just taken a mouthful of burger, so he nodded his head.

When Simon drove Anita home that afternoon, Simon walked into the house with Anita. When Amos saw him, he grunted.

Simon said he had things to do and made an excuse to leave.

Anita wasn't happy with her brother, but because she knew her brother felt bad about Eli leaving, she didn't say anything to him about being so rude.

CHAPTER 17

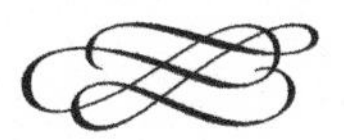

This is the day which the LORD hath made; we will rejoice and be glad in it.
Psalm 118:24

It was weeks later, and the midwife had visited Anita at the house.

"All's well with the *boppli?*" Amos asked after Dora had left.

"Jah, everything is going fine. And she'll

be coming to see me every few days until the birth, since it's so close."

"Gut."

Anita thought about her younger brothers who had left the community. She hadn't seen them in years. She wondered whether they had wives and children, or had remained unmarried. There had been no word from them. It hurt her that they hadn't bothered to keep in touch. She didn't know where they were. They could've called to their parents' old house, or could have written. She glanced over at Amos wondering if he ever thought about his older brothers.

"Simon's coming to dinner," Amos said suddenly.

"Jah, he is. I'm glad you two have sorted out your differences."

Amos stared ahead. "It's sometimes not easy to get along with *familye."*

Anita heard Hannah come back into the house through the back door. She walked into the kitchen and saw Hannah with a bundle of vegetables. "She said everything looks good, Hannah."

"I'm glad. And the space we made for the *boppli* is all ready and waiting."

Hannah and Anita had given Sam's old crib a fresh coat of white paint, and Hannah was nearly finished making the quilt. They'd pushed the double bed over to one side of the bedroom, and there was more than enough room for the crib in Anita's large bedroom.

"I think it'll be a boy," Hannah said.

"It doesn't matter to me."

"Have a lie down, Anita, and then you'll be fresh for Simon's visit."

Anita frowned and looked across the kitchen at Hannah. "*Nee,* I have to help you."

"Off you go." Hannah made shooing motions with both hands. "Both boys are sleeping, so I can get plenty done before they wake up."

"I'll just have a little sleep, then. If that's all right?"

"*Jah.* I want you to be well rested."

Anita walked into her bedroom wondering if Hannah guessed that she was starting to feel fond of Simon. She lay down on her bed; a rest was just what she needed.

When Anita woke, she wasn't sure she hadn't slept the whole night and missed dinner. She walked to the bathroom and splashed cold water on her face, and then headed out to the kitchen.

She opened the door and immediately smelled the roasted chicken and vegetables. Then she heard men's voices in the living room.

"There you are. I was just about to go and wake you," Hannah said.

"Simon's already here?"

"*Jah.* He's in the living room."

Anita looked over at the boys' empty table. "Where are the boys?"

"They're playing out in the living room. Can you tell everyone to come in now? Dinner's ready."

Anita looked at the set table. "You should've woken me sooner."

"Nee."

Anita was nervous about seeing Simon. She told herself not to be silly, and walked into the living room. Simon and Amos rose to their feet when she entered the room.

"Dinner ready?" Amos asked.

"Hello, Anita," Simon said.

"Hello, Simon, and *jah,* dinner is ready."

"Come on, Ben, Sam," Amos called to the boys.

The boys left their wooden toys at the side of the room, and followed them into the kitchen. Anita put the boys' food in front of them, and then sat down at the table.

After the silent prayers were said, Amos rubbed his hands together. "This looks *gut.*"

Simon nodded. "It does, Hannah." He looked at Anita. "And, Anita."

"I'm afraid I was asleep, and left Hannah to cook the dinner all on her own."

"You're not sick, are you?" Simon asked.

Amos said, "The midwife was here to see her, and everything's fine."

Anita nodded.

"I'm happy to hear it. You should come and look at my newly painted rooms."

"You've done it already?" Anita asked.

"I have. And you made a *wunderbaar* choice of color." He looked at Hannah and said, "Why don't you and Anita walk the boys over tomorrow?"

"After the meeting?" Hannah asked.

"I forgot the meeting was on tomorrow. *Jah,* come after the meeting."

Hannah smiled. "We'd like that. We don't visit often enough."

The dinner went without a cross word or

argument. Both Hannah and Amos took the boys upstairs to put them to bed.

"Amos seems to have a different attitude toward me now," Simon said.

"I know he does."

"Have you said anything to him?"

"I've said a lot to him, but I've got no idea what made the difference. Maybe Hannah said something."

They had a few more minutes alone before Hannah and Amos came back down the stairs.

THE NEXT DAY'S gathering was held at Hans Yoder's *haus.* Anita and Hannah had just reached the back row, when Anita felt strong pains.

"I think the *boppli's* coming," she whispered to Hannah.

"What? Now?"

"Jah, I had pains all night, but they were mild so I thought they were nothing. Only now they're getting worse."

"Anita, you should've said something sooner. I'll tell Amos, and then Dora can follow us."

Anita looked over at Dora, who was looking at them and seemed to sense what was going on. When Hannah took the two boys to tell Amos what was happening, Dora hurried over to Anita.

"Is it time?" Anita asked.

"Jah," Dora said. "I think it is. I'll drive you to Amos' house."

Just as they walked out of the house, Simon came running after her. "Anita, are you all right?"

Dora held up her hand in front of his face. "It's her time. It's a time when she needs women around her, not men."

Simon nodded and stepped back. Anita gave him a little smile before Dora had her walking to the buggy.

SIX HOURS LATER, Daniel Joshua Graber was born. Anita held the tiny bundle in her arms and looked down at him. Dora had wrapped him in a white cotton wrap, with nothing showing except his tiny dark-pink hands and his face. Hannah had stayed beside her the whole time.

"He's so beautiful, Anita," Hannah said. "I can't wait for Ben and Sam to get back from *mamm's haus* so they can see him."

"He's a miracle. I can't keep my eyes from him."

The midwife was now busy cleaning up the room. "He's a fine *bu.*"

"I'll tell Amos he's born," Hannah said.

"He would've heard him cry," Dora said bluntly.

Hannah ignored Dora and left the room.

When Hannah came back into the room a moment later, she sat next to Anita. "Amos is excited, and so is Simon."

"Simon's here?"

"He's been here the whole time, waiting with Amos. They'd like to see both of you."

"Let me clean up first," Dora said. "There are some things men were never meant to see."

Hannah and Anita smiled at each other.

Hannah sighed. "Daniel makes me long for another *boppli.*"

"I'm certain you'll have more," Anita said. "Many more."

"Was the birth what you'd thought it would be?" Hannah asked.

"I guess it wasn't too far different than what people had told me. It wasn't as bad as some of them had said."

Dora opened the door that led outside to take a load of things to her buggy. When she came back, she said, "All done. You can let the men in now, if you must."

Hannah opened the door, and called Amos and Simon in. Simon let Amos go ahead of him to get his first look at his nephew.

"I can't let anyone have a hold of him because I can't let go of him just yet," Anita joked.

Amos moved away, and let Simon come forward to see Daniel.

"He's lovely, Anita," Simon said.

Anita stared down at the bundle in her arms. "Yes he is."

"Now is he my nephew once removed, or is it by marriage?" he spoke in a high voice.

Anita laughed at him mimicking Fran. "He's your nephew, and I don't know about the rest. It's too much for me to think about right now."

CHAPTER 18

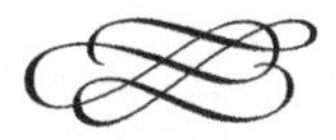

This book of the law shall not depart out of thy mouth; but thou shalt meditate therein day and night, that thou mayest observe to do according to all that is written therein: for then thou shalt make thy way prosperous, and then thou shalt have good success.

Joshua 1:8

Over the next year, life for Anita and Daniel settled into a routine. Simon had gone back to his pattern of having dinner a few times a week at Hannah and Amos' house. He was often included when the family group attended community events, and he and Anita continued to enjoy each other's company.

It was after one of those family dinners that Simon had an opportunity to have a private word with Anita.

"On Tuesday, after Hannah goes to work, Amos will be out working on the farm." He laughed. "I've rehearsed this, and now I can't remember what I'm supposed to say."

Anita smiled. "Just say it plainly."

"I want you to come somewhere with me; you and Daniel."

"Aren't you supposed to be working, telling your men what to do?"

"I'm the boss. They can do without me for one day. I want to take Daniel on his first outing."

"He's been on lots of outings."

"Not with me. I'll take him on his first buggy ride in *my* buggy."

Anita giggled, and nodded. "I'll look forward to it."

They were interrupted when Amos came back into the room.

"What were you two talking about?"

Anita and Simon looked at each other, and Amos raised his hands. "Don't tell me." Amos sat down shaking his head.

Simon left not long after that, and Anita went into her room. She stared at her sleeping baby. Anita was excited about seeing Simon the next day and wanted to share it with someone, but there was no one to tell.

She leaned over and whispered to Daniel,

who had just moved into his big boy's bed, "I'll never let you forget your *Dat.* Joshua is your *vadder,* and when you get bigger, I've got so many stories I can tell you about him."

She leaned down close to his face and kissed him gently on his soft cheek before changing into her nightgown and getting into her own bed.

THE NEXT DAY, they were with Simon in his buggy. "And where are we going? Can you tell me yet?"

"I'm going to take you both on a picnic."

"Daniel and I love picnics."

Simon stopped the buggy between his place and Amos' house. He led them to the place where they'd run into each other not long after she'd arrived. She'd been making daisy chains and he'd been checking on his fences.

He had a blanket spread out already and a large picnic basket was on one side. There were limp daisy chains on the blanket. He picked one up, and laughed. "They didn't look like this when I made them yesterday."

"You made them yesterday, and they've had no water?" Anita laughed at him. "It was so nice of you to do this for us." She looked down at Daniel who had recently had his first birthday. "Say '*denke, Onkel* Simon.'"

Daniel waved his arms and jabbered a few sounds in response, trying to decide if he liked crawling on the ground.

"I didn't do it for Daniel. Although it was nice of him to join us." He stared into her eyes. "I did it for you. Let's sit."

Anita was pleased. She smiled at him when they'd sat down, and then she looked away.

"Do you think that Amos is right about our age difference?" Simon asked.

"*Jah*, you're far too old for me. I need to look for someone younger."

"I'm serious, Anita."

Anita gulped as she looked into his eyes. The joking was over. He was being serious, and she knew she had to give a straightforward answer. "I think age doesn't matter. It might matter if it were a large age gap or if the younger person was still a teenager, but a slight difference shouldn't be a problem."

"Do you remember the list that Fran gave you a long time ago?"

"*Jah*. I don't think I'll ever forget Fran's list."

He pulled the paper out of his pocket.

She stared at the paper. "You kept it?"

He nodded.

"I wondered where it got to."

He held the paper in one hand, and with the other hand reached into the basket and pulled out a pin. "I need to ask you an important question, Anita Graber."

Anita's heart pounded. Was he going to ask her to marry him? She realized she wanted him to.

When he hesitated, she asked, "What question?"

He smiled. "I've added my name to Fran's list."

Anita put her hand to her mouth and giggled.

"I was hoping that you might take this piece of paper and this pin, and if you happen to stick the pin in my name, I'm hoping you'll agree to marry me."

"And what if the pin sticks in someone else's name?"

"You won't have to marry him. We won't let him know about it, but if you do stick the pin in my name, you'll have to marry me. What do you say?"

"This is a big decision. And we're leaving it up to chance?"

"We're leaving it up to *Gott.* This is how

the bishops are chosen. Well, not with a pin, but by lot, which is a similar principle."

"Are you prepared for the outcome?" Anita's heart pounded hard against her chest.

"More than prepared. I've been thinking for a long time about asking you to marry me, but at the same time giving you a way out."

Anita stretched out her hand. "Give me the paper."

"You have to close your eyes, and I'll put the pin and the paper in your hands when you tell me you're ready."

"Since when do you make all the rules?"

"Shh. This is my idea, so I make the rules. Now close your eyes and tell me when you're ready."

"Okay, but you have to keep an eye on Daniel. He's been trying to walk, and I don't want to miss his first steps." She glanced down at Daniel who was sitting next to her, playing happily with the limp daisy chains.

Then she closed her eyes and silently prayed that *Gott* would help her choose his name if he were the man for her. And she hoped that he was. She left it in *Gott's* hands, and without opening her eyes, said, "I'm ready."

She placed her hands out and Simon carefully placed the pin between the thumb and forefinger of her right hand, and then placed the paper in her other hand.

"Now I've unfolded the paper, and it's the right side up. You've got no idea where I could've put my name. I don't want you to think I've put it at the bottom."

"Which is the top and which is the bottom?"

"I've handed it to you with the top at the top, and the bottom at the bottom."

"And what happens if I don't stick the pin in your name?"

"Everything in life can't be planned, Anita. Sometimes you have to take chances."

With her eyes still closed, she nodded.

She placed the paper down in front of her on the blanket, circled the pin and then pushed the pin into the paper. When he remained silent, she was certain that she's missed his name. "Can I open my eyes now?"

"Jah."

Anita opened her eyes and looked down at the list. She saw that it wasn't Fran's list at all, and what's more, every spot on the page held Simon's name. She looked up at him and laughed. "I knew it."

"Nee you didn't."

"Jah, I thought you might have done something like that."

He leaned over. "Will you marry me, Anita Graber?"

She nodded. "I will."

He leaned over and gently pressed his lips against hers.

"I have to marry you now. I said I would if the pin stuck you."

"You're exactly right."

They both laughed, and Daniel clapped his hands and joined in.

"When do you think we should tell Amos and Hannah?" Anita asked, wondering what their reactions would be.

"A year or two."

"That's most likely for the best," Anita said. "But who knows what man Fran will try and make me marry before then."

"Perhaps we should marry as soon as we can?"

Anita nodded. "Perhaps."

"I do have that list, you know - Fran's list - the real one. I kept it as a reminder."

Anita laughed. "A reminder of what?"

"A reminder that I shouldn't let you out of my sight for too long." He smiled at her. "You're the only woman I've ever been able to talk to."

Anita's face hurt from smiling so much. "Really?"

"*Jah.* I knew there was something about

you from the moment I first saw you walk into the kitchen at Amos and Hannah's house."

"I felt a certain fondness toward you too, back then, but it seemed no one else thought we'd make a match."

He took hold of her hand. "It never matters what others think. We're the ones who have to live our lives. As long as we're not hurting other people, it shouldn't matter who we love."

"It doesn't matter. You can remember to say all that when we go back to the *haus* to tell Amos."

Simon cleared his throat. "I'll let you do the talking."

"The one who does the asking is the one who has to do the talking. You asked me to marry you, so you have to tell Amos."

He pulled a sad face. "Okay." He leaned down and kissed Daniel on top of his head.

"I'll hold Daniel in my arms while I tell him, so Amos can't hit me."

"That's not a bad idea." Anita thought back to the old man on the bus who'd given her words of comfort over a year ago. As he'd promised, time had made things easier. She no longer dwelt on trying to figure out why Joshua was taken from her. For Daniel, she had to live in the present and be happy. God had given her Simon now, a wonderful man to be happy with, and God had blessed her with a son. How could she be sad any longer?

After they enjoyed some private time together, Anita and Simon, and Daniel went back that evening to tell Hannah and Amos their news.

Truly my soul waiteth upon God: from him cometh my salvation. He only is my rock and my salvation; he is my defence; I shall not be greatly moved.

Psalm 62:1

Thank you for reading Amish Widow's Hope.

www.SamanthaPriceAuthor.com

THE NEXT BOOK IN THE SERIES

Book 2

The Pregnant Amish Widow

When Grace's abusive husband died, she couldn't wait to return to her Amish community. Soon, Grace found out her old crush was still single. She had high hopes for marriage with someone who wasn't going to terrorise her as her late husband had. But with younger women vying for her his attention, would he give a pregnant widow a second thought?

ALL SAMANTHA PRICE'S SERIES

Amish Maids Trilogy
A 3 book Amish romance series of novels featuring 5 friends finding love.

Amish Love Blooms
A 6 book Amish romance series of novels about four sisters and their cousins.

Amish Misfits
A series of 7 stand-alone books about people who have never fitted in.

The Amish Bonnet Sisters
To date there are 28 books in this continuing family saga. My most popular and best-selling series.

Amish Women of Pleasant Valley
An 8 book Amish romance series with the same characters. This has been one of my most popular series.

Ettie Smith Amish Mysteries
An ongoing cozy mystery series with octogenarian sleuths. Popular with lovers of mysteries such as Miss Marple or Murder She Wrote.

Amish Secret Widows' Society
A ten novella mystery/romance series - a prequel to the Ettie Smith Amish Mysteries.

Expectant Amish Widows

A stand-alone Amish romance series of 19 books.

Seven Amish Bachelors
A 7 book Amish Romance series following the Fuller brothers' journey to finding love.

Amish Foster Girls
A 4 book Amish romance series with the same characters who have been fostered to an Amish family.

Amish Brides
An Amish historical romance. 5 book series with the same characters who have arrived in America to start their new life.

Amish Romance Secrets
The first series I ever wrote. 6 novellas following the same characters.

Amish Christmas Books

Each year I write an Amish Christmas stand-alone romance novel.

Amish Twin Hearts
A 4 book Amish Romance featuring twins and their friends.

Amish Wedding Season
The second series I wrote. It has the same characters throughout the 5 books.

Gretel Koch Jewel Thief
A clean 5 book suspense/mystery series about a jewel thief who has agreed to consult with the FBI.